PRAISE f(

"Seniors Sleuth is a delightful whodunit filled with colorful senior citizens, numerous red herrings, and even a little dash of romance for our earnest rookie investigator, Winston Wong. A charming cozy debut that will keep you guessing until the very end."

> —Sarah M. Chen, author of "Canyon Ladies" in the Sisters in Crime/LA's anthology, *LAdies Night*

"J.J. Chow entices mystery readers with her fledgling 'senior' detective. Winston Wong finds himself sought out by aging baby-boomers because of a typo in his *Pennysaver* ad. Luckily his first client has a stunning granddaughter and he needs the money. What follows is more than Winston bargained for--a murder investigation at the Sweet Breeze Care Facility. Winston's love of video games aids him in pursuing the truth about Joseph Sawyer's death and the author's clear, precise prose puts the reader into the story fast and carries through to the end."

> —Gay Degani, author of the literary suspense, *What Came Before*

"Winston Wong is not your conventional private detective. For a start, he's a video game nerd and on the wrong side of forty with very few prospects on the romance front. Not only that, Winston's first case investigating the demise of a ninety-year old man looks like a non-starter. But Winston is determined to make a success of his new career and soon discovers that it's not just death that roams the corridors of Sweet Breeze retirement home.

Chow's work in geriatric welfare provides an intriguing backdrop that she skillfully weaves into her clever plot. *Seniors Sleuth* is written with warmth, humor and an eccentric cast of characters and, most of all, a loveable hero. It's a breath of fresh air to what I hope will become a continuing series."

> —Hannah Dennison, author of *The Honeychurch Hall Mysteries* and *The Vicky Hill Mysteries*

"Winston Wong, a slacker game developer in the middle of Silicon Valley, is a completely charming rookie sleuth. His modern high-tech world intersects the old, as Winston finds himself embroiled in a suspicious death at a senior home. J.J. Chow adds a fresh, original voice to the mystery genre! I can't wait to read more of Winston's adventures."

—Naomi Hirahara, Edgar Award-winning author of the Mas Arai and Officer Ellie Rush mysteries

"*Seniors Sleuth* is a charming, humorous novel with an intriguing storyline wrapped with endearing characters. It's a total enjoyment to read."

—Lois Lavrisa, bestselling award-winning author of *Dying for Dinner Rolls*

SENIORS
SLEUTH
a Winston Wong mystery

J.J. Chow

IN MEMORY OF MY MOTHER,

who introduced me to Agatha Christie's books

CHAPTER 1

WINSTON SQUINTED AT the fine print and scowled. The *Pennysaver* ad was printed as "Winston Wong, Senior*s* Sleuth," not "Winston Wong, Senior Sleuth." The word "senior" was supposed to make him seem more experienced; after all, he didn't want to sound like a noob at the detecting game. Due to the error, he now seemed lame, ready to mooch off older adults for some dough.

He picked up the phone to call the company and correct it, but then he thought, *Screw it.* Instead, he rubbed his slight potbelly to bring in the clients. Whenever his sister Marcy saw him, she teased, "Looks more like the lucky Buddha's every day." In fact, he'd had to up the size of his pants, which he now wore baggy-style like a punk kid because of his expanding waist. At least the style matched his flip-flops.

Winston swiveled in his black mesh computer chair and surveyed the office. *Not a bad look for the mother-in-law unit.* With no wife and family to speak of, the spare room used to be his man cave. But he had swept all the consoles and accompanying video games into the main house in preparation for his new business, leaving only two electric blue inflatable chairs. They would serve as seats for his future clients, but he had made them classy by draping them with faux leather throws.

He tapped his fingers on the scarred particleboard folding table and looked at his clunky laptop. Maybe he could play a quick game of *Minesweeper* first, without getting sucked in (as usual). Before he could even touch the keyboard, the door swung open.

In walked fire on stilettos. The woman's waterfall of flaming curls tumbled onto a gold gown welded onto her curves. Her sapphire eyes, which had a slight Eurasian tilt, pierced him. "Are you Winston Wong?"

He couldn't move.

"Seniors Sleuth?" she asked.

Winston swallowed, the saliva making his throat feel even drier. He smoothed his part to the left to better cover his blinding bald forehead. "Yes, that's me."

"I've been looking for you."

Winston had trouble finding his voice. Before he could even respond, she turned and left. He thought he had missed his chance, but to his relief, she soon returned…ushering in an old woman wearing an outrageous frilly muumuu. The scent of apples and cinnamon lingered in the air. Maybe she was the kind of old lady who baked goodies for her grandchildren in her spare time.

At second glance, though, the warm associations faded. Ice exuded from Granny's face. Her hair appeared colorless, and her dull blue eyes were bleached versions of her granddaughter's sparkling ones. Granny's gaze floated, detached from everything around the room.

"I'm Carmen Solstice," the knockout beauty said. "My grandmother's Eve." She turned toward the old woman, raising her voice. "Nana, this is the nice detective I told you about, Winston Wong."

Eve didn't stop her roaming eyes.

Carmen brushed her slender hand against her grandmother's shoulder. "He's here to help you. He'll figure out what happened to Teddy."

At the name, Eve covered her face with her gnarled hands and moaned. "Teddy, Teddy. Why did they kill you?"

Carmen shushed her grandmother, making soothing noises until Nana became distant again. She walked her grandmother over to the far wall. "Why don't you take a look at this, uh, artwork while the detective and I chat?"

Winston smacked his palm against his forehead. He had forgotten to remove the framed equation reading, "I like to eat = area of a circle divided by radius squared." It didn't even have a picture of a steaming pie to help the old woman out. Unless she liked mathematics, Nana would be occupied for a while.

When Carmen returned, Winston asked, "Um, what's this talk about a killing?" He didn't want his first case to be a homicide.

"Don't worry," she said, rolling her eyes. She glanced back at her grandmother, scooted closer to Winston, and whispered, "It's all a figment of her imagination. Nana suffers from dementia. Teddy, my gramps, has been gone for decades, and he died quite peacefully in his sleep."

"So what do you need me for then?"

"Well, Nana took a liking to one of her co-residents at the care facility and confused him with her long-lost husband. This other 'Teddy' died yesterday afternoon, and she keeps thinking that it's foul play. It's really stressing her out, so I want you to investigate"—Carmen used air quotation marks around the word—"and settle the matter."

"I don't understand. Can't you just provide her with the original of Teddy's death certificate?"

Carmen frowned, a cute pull of her lips. "We don't have the documentation anymore, and I can't be bothered getting a copy from a governmental office. They're always so slow."

"What about showing her the new death certificate?"

"The replacement gramps was called Joseph, so that won't work. She'll see the new name and be even more confused."

Winston leaned back in his chair, making it squeak. "Let me get this straight. You want me to stage an investigation to show your grandmother that her Teddy died naturally, so she can move on."

"Exactly." Carmen leaned forward, her juicy strawberry lips an inch away from his. "I'll pay you, of course." She pulled two crisp fifties from a miniscule purse. Where had she hidden that on her body? "Will this be enough, or do you need more?"

Winston watched Carmen's fingers dance close to him with the money and gulped. "That's plenty. It's not even a real case after all."

"Good. It's settled then." Carmen wrote down the address on a piece of paper. Even her writing curled in seductive flourishes. "Sweet Breeze. 2255 Julian Street." Winston watched Carmen's hips sway away from him as she helped her grandmother out the door.

CHAPTER 2

AN IMPOSING BLUE Victorian house, complete with multiple gables and bay windows, housed the Sweet Breeze Residential Care Facility. The neighboring residences were turned into businesses as well, showcasing a Jane Marshall, D.D.S., Boyle & Davies Law Offices, and Hair Solutions Salon. A treasure trove of services close by for the aged residents.

Wicker chairs dotted Sweet Breeze's round porch, but nobody sat there. Probably because downtown San Jose traffic wasn't very scenic. A slew of billboards nearby marred the cloudless sky: Baskin-Robbins, Sana Technologies, and the KRCT radio station.

Despite the congested surroundings, it was still a grand home. He wouldn't mind living there himself—if his sister hadn't just sprung for the house he'd been renting for the last ten years. It's an investment, Marcy had said. She didn't like speaking directly. She would never call it bailing him out.

At the door, Winston paused. He saw the octagonal *bat gua* above the frame and knew that the home was owned by some superstitious Chinese folks. Who else would place the protective mirror to ward off evil spirits? They probably had the whole place feng shui'ed before opening up their business. It was a good thing the ninety-year-old man had died peacefully. Otherwise, the owners would have a fit.

Winston walked inside and immediately smelled an infusion of mothballs. Close to the entrance behind a wide sideboard, a nurse with white scrubs filled Dixie cups with various pills. A line of patients waited before her. She handed the first one his marked cup and waited until he had swallowed, before swiveling her body toward the open front door.

Her single raven braid almost swung at Winston as she turned to face him. Her face, uncovered by makeup, displayed crow's feet and slight laugh lines, and Winston estimated her to be thirty-five. Five years younger than his own age.

Her cool mocha eyes assessed him. "Are you looking for a place for a family member or a friend?"

"Neither."

"Well, you're a little too early for yourself."

A sense of humor. She turned her attention back to the little cups and didn't see his smile. Winston pulled out a business card from his wallet, a flimsy rectangular piece of paper he'd printed at home. It had the essentials, though: home address, mobile number, email. He tapped her shoulder and handed it over.

She raised an eyebrow. "*Senior* Sleuth, huh? I didn't know there were different levels of investigators."

He wasn't sure if she was teasing him or not, but he puffed out his chest anyway. "I'm here on official business, I'll have you know. The granddaughter of Eve Solstice hired me to investigate the death of Joseph."

Her eyes clouded at the mention of the deceased, and she fingered a delicate chain at her neck, hidden beneath her uniform.

"Can you help me out?" Winston asked.

Shaking her head, she pointed at the plastic tag pinned to her shirt: Kristy Blake, RN. "You probably want to talk to the administrator, Rob Turner. He's holed upstairs, like usual. Only comes down during his obligatory smoke break. First door on the left."

"Thanks." Winston huffed his way up the long flight of polished cherry wood steps. How were the residents ever able to meet face-to-face with this man? The administrator's door was closed when he arrived, so he knocked hard against the thick wood.

"Hold on a sec." Winston heard some shuffling from inside. "Okay, I'm ready."

A young man sprouting an unruly mop of straw hair sat behind a paper-infested desk. His cat-green eyes, encased in wire frames, flicked between his computer screen and Winston in an unsettling ping-pong motion. He waved Winston in, gesturing to a cushioned mahogany chair. "Sit down."

"I'm here to investigate a case," Winston said, as he placed a business card in Rob's hand.

The administrator frowned, his full attention on Winston now. "What about?"

"I want to conduct a search into the death of one of your residents. Joseph?"

"Joseph Sawyer? Yeah, he died two days ago." Rob narrowed at his eyes at Winston. "What's wrong? It said natural causes on his death certificate."

"I understand that," Winston said. "Carmen, the granddaughter of your resident Eve Solstice, wants to do a mock investigation to help her grandmother feel better about the death."

"Ah, Carmen." Rob's eyes unfocused as he smiled.

It seemed Carmen cast her sensual spell on all men around her. Winston cleared his throat. "Anyway, it appears that Eve suffers from dementia and thought that Joseph was her husband. She would feel better to have a formal declaration that he died naturally."

"I see. Eve's delusions shouldn't be catered to, though. She'll soon forget all the fuss, and Joe had no close family, so it's not really a big concern for anyone." Rob took off his glasses and rubbed his eyes. "Besides, it'll be a bother for me and the residents, having a stranger around."

It's my first paying case, Winston wanted to say, but Rob seemed ready to boot him out of the office. Winston looked around the room to find something to distract the administrator. His eyes traveled past a wilting potted plant, a hefty filing cabinet, and a glass case filled with medication. He looked up and spotted an *Eternals* comic book framed on the wall.

"Hey, the Eternals. Great stuff. What I wouldn't give to be near immortal."

"Huh?" Rob followed Winston's gaze. "Oh yeah, I love The Forgotten One."

"His superhuman strength rivals Thor and Hercules."

Rob grinned. "It's good to find another comic book aficionado. Are you going to Comic-Con?"

"Maybe," Winston said. Probably not, though. He couldn't afford a ticket to San Diego on his budget, especially with this current gig swirling down the drain.

Rob looked back at his computer. "Well, nice talking to you, but duty calls."

Winston caught the screen's reflection off Rob's glasses. It wasn't text but moving images. "Are you playing a video game?"

"No." Rob coughed. "I'm looking over financial documents."

Winston saw him jab at a couple of buttons to close down the program. He must have pressed a wrong key because a barrage of laser sounds filled the air.

The noises seemed familiar. "Is that...*Space Domination*?"

"You know it?" Rob asked.

"Sure do. Tested that MMO for four months straight."

"Really? You work in the industry?"

Winston massaged his temples. "I was a game tester for a really long time." Until the switch to detective work.

"That's so cool," Rob said. "You want a drink? I've got a mini fridge under the desk." He ducked below the table, and Winston could hear the door hiss open.

"All I've got is Sprite left." He pulled out a Swiss Army knife with a bottle opener and popped the top off. "I only get the good stuff, the kind that comes in glass bottles. Aluminum and plastic throw off the taste. Want some?"

Rob grabbed a foam cup from a nearby stack and offered it, but Winston refused. "No, I'm more of a Coke man myself."

"Well said." Rob took a swig of clear soda straight from the bottle. "I always wanted to make video games, but my parents shut me down. Mom's a bookkeeper and Pop's an accountant, so they wanted something more 'stable.' That's how I got roped in here."

"Your mom and dad pushed you to work in a senior home?"

"No, I hopped around doing odd jobs, hoping for a break into video games, but my folks demanded I take night classes on finance. Dad always says, 'There's nothing certain in life except death and taxes.' So I decided on death when I heard about the open administrator position here." Rob tapped his noggin. "I exaggerated my education a bit saying I was pursuing an MBA, and that Chinese Richie Rich owner was desperate to hire. Here I am two years later. I'd love to change jobs, but it's all about connections. Or moolah."

Rob stared at Winston for a moment. "Do you still have ties to the gaming industry?"

"Sure," Winston said. Sort of. He did have a friend who owned a recording studio and provided voice actors for games. And he still received queries to test for companies now and then. "You have to start low and move your way up, though."

Rob waved the comment away. "Nah, I have management experience now. I figure I could be a producer pretty quick. Will you put in a good word for me?"

"I can try," Winston said. He didn't want to blast the kid's hopes right away. Guys with no experience ended up testing, and that usually led to a dead end. That was how Winston's life had turned out, after all. Of course, if his dot-com investments had worked out... But it was over ten years later, and he still hadn't sorted out the financial mess.

"Thanks, buddy," Rob said. "I think you can start this phony investigation of yours. You scratch my back, and I'll scratch yours."

CHAPTER 3

WINSTON HEADED BACK downstairs into the main
lobby of Sweet Breeze. The nurse must have finished
with her medication dispensation because the area lay
open and empty. The high-vaulted room reminded him more of a
swanky hotel than an old people's home. It boasted plush cream
carpeting, unmarked by a single stain, and its fluffiness sprung
back after every silenced step. Potted plants in gold containers
sprinkled the room, their glossy leaves so surreal that he had to
touch one to make sure it was genuine. A microsuede couch cozied
up to matching armchairs in the room's center. They faced a
burnished mahogany upright piano. At the rear of the house,
through an automatic sliding door, he caught a glimpse of a flower
garden lined with concrete benches and a porcelain birdbath.

A soft tinkling sounded from one of the many identical rooms
to the side of the living area. The doors were all the same, solid
imposing ones with stained glass inserts. The merry jingle came
from a miniature gold wind chime attached to a door on his left.

Out of it flowed a swath of deep purple, a silk monster ready
to swallow him up. He spied a tiny head peeping out from the
great folds of fabric, gaunt but regal in its bearing. The woman,
with high cheekbones and a straight nose, was covered in long
scarves of varying purple hues. She stretched out the tips of her
fingers to greet him.

"Hello, my dear." She extended the syllables, singing the words. With a wave of a hand, she fluttered a scarf away, exposing an arm. The bony hand, bejeweled in rhinestones, dangled in front of his nose. "I'm Anastasia Templeton."

He decided to play along with her ladylike persona. He brushed his lips against her twig-like fingers. "Pleased to meet you, Anastasia. My name's Winston."

"Pray tell, what are you doing in our fine home? I haven't seen you here before."

"I'm a private investigator, hired by Eve Solsti— are you all right?" The woman had flopped one hand against her forehead, emitting a theatrical sigh.

"Eve Solstice." Anastasia spat the name out with disgust. "That woman is trouble, and she doesn't belong here with us more *capable* residents." She tapped her own head with emphasis. "Anyway, do go on."

Winston cleared his throat. "I'm actually here by her granddaughter's request to look into the death of Joseph Sawyer."

"Nonsense. Whatever for?"

He was taught to never lie to his elders. "You see, Joseph reminded Eve of her husband. I need to look into the affair, verify the natural cause of death, and calm her nerves."

Anastasia made a dismissive noise. "Eve hounded the gentle soul. Joe was a saint with that crazy woman. He played along with her antics, talking and spending time with her at all hours. I even caught him patting her hand once or twice. Sometimes I think she exaggerated her memory problems just to get closer to the poor man. She drove him to the grave."

Winston spluttered. "Do you think there's something unusual about his death?" Anastasia fiddled with her amethyst earring, squeezing it between her thumb and forefinger. She yanked it loose by accident. Winston peered at her earlobe.

"I'm fine. It's just a clip-on." Anastasia opened her hand to show him, and he noticed that a cracked purple gem lay on her palm.

"Did Joe's death upset you?"

"No, no." Anastasia shook her head hard, and the massive pearl strand on her neck jiggled. "He was ninety, and that's knocking at the gates of heaven."

Loud, insistent piano music broke up their conversation. "It's Jazzman," Anastasia shouted over the playing, before she waltzed over to the upright.

While conversing with her, Winston had failed to notice a resident enter the center space. Now a black man sat on the polished bench, hunched over the ivory keys, running his fingers along the piano's spine. The man was dressed up, dapper in a white button-down shirt and a gray silk vest. No sheet music before him. Only a black top hat rested on the piano lid. Winston watched, amazed, as the music swirled around him, filling the room with its pulsing notes. Several times, the melody paused but then resurrected again. In the end, the man swiveled around, a blinding grin stuck on his face. He bowed with a flourish of the top hat. A hearty clapping came from behind Winston. He turned to see the nurse Kristy entering the room, and he echoed her sincere applause.

"Ladies, what did you think?" Jazzman's cool bass voice penetrated the room.

"Marvelous," Anastasia said. She sidled up to the player and her body half-rested against the piano, leaning in toward him.

"Wonderful as always, Jazzman," Kristy said.

His dark eyes glinted at the women's compliments. Then he looked at Winston. "What does the gentleman think?"

"I'm not a connoisseur of jazz music," Winston said, "but I really enjoyed it."

"Fair enough," Jazzman said. "Not everybody is blessed with the gift of musical appreciation." Winston wondered what Jazzman would say if he knew that Winston liked old love ballads circa Johnny Mathis.

"I take it that Rob approved the investigation," Kristy said to Winston. She introduced the two men to one another, explaining Winston's presence in the facility. "I'll leave you two alone to chat."

Jazzman watched Kristy walk away. "That lady's one hotsy-totsy dame. It's a shame she's still single."

Winston corralled his thoughts. "Jazzman, tell me about Joseph."

Jazzman snorted. "He was a piano hog. It's good to have this baby to myself now." He ran his fingers along the zebra keys, conjuring a soft hiss of music. "The man wouldn't stop butting in and playing the only song he knew, the same intro melody to 'Für Elise,' over and over again." Jazzman shrugged. "Besides that, Joe was all right. Not a snazzy dresser, though, always walking about in sweats and such. Don't know what the ladies saw in him."

"You mean Eve Solstice, right?"

Jazzman shook his head. "No, all the women chatted with him. He's so 'nice and friendly,' they said. Eve, of course, clung to him, claiming that he was her husband. Anastasia followed him, too, trying to work her charms on the guy. Of course, she does that to any male who breathes." Anastasia sniffed at Jazzman and moved away from the bench. "Kristy, too, had a soft spot for Joe. It must have been all those bags they hooked him up to for dialysis."

"He does sound like he was pretty sick and up there in age…"

"I know where you're going with this," Jazzman said. "His death was all natural. You'll be done with this case by the day's end. So you want to hear me play some more? I do a mean Chick Corea." Jazzman stretched his fingers and wiggled them.

"How did you learn to play?" Winston asked. "It's inspiring to watch, especially since you don't use sheet music."

"You follow your soul in jazz. All those papers just mess with the beat in your mind." He smoothed one hand over his hair, its curly white mass shorn short. "I can't remember a time I didn't play. My parents started me the minute I could sit down at the bench. You know, I was named after the great Count Basie."

"Who was he?"

Jazzman shook his head. "Count Basie did everything in the world of jazz. Pianist, organist, bandleader, and composer. What couldn't that cat do? He led his jazz orchestra for almost fifty years. My legal name's Basie Jones, but Jazzman's the name I adopted for radio."

Winston studied Jazzman's neat appearance. A natural performer. "I can picture you doing that, though I think TV would have worked even better."

Jazzman chuckled. "If only. I wanted to be famous, a great jazz pianist, but my hands were shot. I blame it on genetics, getting arthritis at an early age. I couldn't play professionally—too hard on the joints—so I got a job spinning records at the radio station. Soon I headed up the night show for the local jazz station. And voilà! Jazzman. Ooh, the ladies loved the sound of that. I worked until the station ran out of funding." He sighed. "Nobody appreciates good music anymore."

Jazzman turned toward the piano and played a bluesy tune.

Kristy walked back into the room then and paused before the piano. "You sound like you need a hug, Jazzman." She gave him a quick embrace, and his melody shifted to an upbeat version.

She turned toward Winston. "Now it's my turn. I can take a quick coffee break and answer any questions you might have."

CHAPTER 4

KRISTY AND WINSTON settled themselves in a tiny alcove. He bet it'd been a closet in the house's original floor plan. The room held a card table, two folding chairs, and a coffeemaker. On the wall a flyer written in legalese talked about cutbacks in employee benefits. A burnt coffee aroma filled the small space.

"You weren't kidding when you said you were going on a coffee break, huh? That's all the food you seem to have here."

"The coffee's not as bad as it smells. You just need to add lots of creamer." She took a foam cup from the stack on the table—those must be everywhere in this place, in Rob's office and now in the break room. She lifted up the coffeepot. "Want a cup?"

"Nah, I swore off the stuff."

"Really?" She poured one for herself. "I couldn't survive a day without this miracle worker."

"I used to drink caffeine all the time, in various forms—tea, coffee, energy shots—in my previous life. Now it's only the occasional cola."

Kristy pressed her fingers against her temples, like she was a carnival mind reader. "The picture's clearing for me. You used to be a vending machine mechanic. That's how you got all the caffeine perks. I wouldn't mind having one of those fancy machines here, piping out hot cappuccinos."

"I only wish," Winston said. "At least, I would have gotten some exercise, checking all those machines." He gave his stomach a love pat. "Nope, I chose to stare at monitors and test video games."

She didn't shudder, like most women who heard about his past profession. Maybe she'd grown up in the Bay Area and was used to computer geeks. "You're not running out the door. Are you impressed by my mad skills?"

"I can understand going into computer games," she said. "I still have my vintage Atari system at home, complete with *Frogger* and *Pitfall*. My Granny and Grampa got it for me." A flicker of sorrow passed across her face. She put some creamer into her coffee and took time swirling it around. "I work with seniors because of my grandparents. I didn't like the way they were treated at their nursing home, so I make sure I take quality care of my patients."

"Like Joseph Sawyer?" Winston asked. He didn't like seeing sadness etched on her capable face, even in passing. Plus, he really did need to know more about the dead man.

"I can't believe Joe's gone. Just the other day he mentioned how his hair was starting to cover his eyes and how he was looking forward to our monthly salon outing."

"I'm sorry," Winston said. "Can you tell me a little bit about the day he died?"

"Yes, I was the one who found Joe's body. I stripped his sheets down. Bagged everything and placed it in the dumpster outside." She shivered and warmed her hands around her steaming beverage. "Joe had a hard time here. He was on peritoneal dialysis because of his kidneys, but he took it like a champ."

"What does peri-whatever mean?"

"Well, kidneys do a lot for your body: they excrete waste, secrete hormones, control your pH, and regulate blood pressure. Since Joe's kidneys didn't work well, he had to have those things done for him. Peritoneal dialysis means that he had a permanent tube placed in his abdomen. A special solution was given to him via that tube, which his body processed, and then the waste got drained out. I exchanged the bags four times a day."

"Wow," he said. Winston decided she must be one tough woman. "Props to you."

"No, the accolades go to Joe. The man was a real sweetheart. He was the genuine article, and there was not one mean bone about him."

Winston remembered what Anastasia had said about Joe putting up with Eve's delusion that he was her husband. "What about with Eve? Did he seem overwhelmed by her need for him? Anastasia mentioned that it was Eve's persistence that 'drove him to his grave.'"

Kristy snorted. "That Anastasia sure is something. She's probably still jealous of Joe's attentions toward Eve. Anastasia wants the focus of any man to be on her. Do you know she thinks she descended from royalty, from the original lost Russian princess herself?"

"I didn't know that, but it would explain the swaths of royal purple and the inordinate amount of jewelry weighing down her body."

Kristy finished her brew of creamer disguised as coffee with a satisfied slurp. "Everyone liked Joe," she said. "Except for Pete Russell, of course."

"Who's that?"

"Our loveable grump-in-residence," she said. "Pete hates everybody here. It probably has to do with his experience in the Vietnam War. Want to meet him?"

Better sooner than later. "I'm game," Winston said.

CHAPTER 5

WINSTON SAW PETE Russell covered up with a wool blanket despite the eighty-degree weather outside, sitting rigid against the back of his hospital bed. The humongous contraption stood out—modern and ugly—against the rest of the room's ornate elegance.

Slender-legged thrones with velvet upholstery flanked a tiny pedestal table balancing on clawed feet. An ancient vanity hid in the corner. Winston noticed Pete had flung a cargo jacket across its mirror, hiding the reflecting surface. Rich redness characterized every corner, from the soft fabric surfaces to the ruby grain of the wooden furniture. Even the wallpaper boasted a scarlet hue.

Kristy sat down in one of the refined chairs, and Winston took the other. Afraid of breaking it, he hovered above its expensive surface. Kristy leaned forward. "Pete, may we interrupt you for a minute?"

The man didn't look up. Spread along his brown blanket was a game of solitaire. Pete had stacked up three piles from ace to king already. He finished the fourth set before he turned his attention toward the nurse.

"I'm done now, Nurse Blake. What do you want?" The man glared at Winston, his coal black eyes a sharp contrast to his buzz-cut snow-white hair. "What's he doing here?"

"You know you can call me Kristy. We don't use formalities at Sweet Breeze. This man's Winston Wong, a private investigator. He's here to look into Joe's death and soothe Eve's mind."

"Everybody made an uncalled for fuss over Joe's death. Especially that Eve woman, what with checking his vital signs and sobbing over the body." Pete's thin lips seemed to disappear into his stolid, square face. "Well, good riddance, I say."

Winston saw Kristy's jaw tighten, but in a sweet voice, she asked, "Why would you say that, Pete?"

"Call me Mr. Russell." He seemed like the kind of man who would prefer titles. "Everybody thinks that Joe was some sort of saint. I don't think so. Why else would his wife leave him? Everyone's got secrets if you dig deep enough."

Kristy clutched the sides of the antique chair until her knuckles turned white. She didn't seem to want to talk anymore, so Winston said, "Why don't we let Nurse Blake finish her duties with the other residents?" He gestured to Pete's blanket. "It's warm outside, Mr. Russell. We can take a walk to the back garden and discuss things man-to-man."

The veteran's eyes grew even darker, and he clipped out his words. "Are you making fun of me?"

"What?" Winston looked to Kristy for help as she let out a soft moan.

Pete threw off his blanket to reveal two stumps where his legs would have been, and his blue-backed bicycle cards scattered all over the room. Pete gestured to the vanity table, where underneath the massive cargo jacket a pair of plastic toes peeped out. "Yeah," he said. "Let's go run a marathon while we're at it."

Prostheses. "I really didn't know," Winston said. "I didn't mean to—"

"Get out!" Pete tossed a remaining card from his bed at Winston. It sliced through the air, like a martial arts trick, and nicked Winston's neck. He felt a sharp stab of pain.

Winston and Kristy both retreated out of the room. With the door closed, she turned toward him. "I'm sorry about that. I should have told you he was a double amputee. He's really sensitive about his legs."

Winston didn't tell Kristy that when he had noticed the prostheses, he had seen something else in Pete's cargo jacket. A slender black handle sticking out of the coat pocket. The slim, deadly outline of a stiletto under the fabric. Pete could have tossed that, instead of a paper card, at him.

Winston must have looked shaken, because Kristy placed one hand on his shoulder. It felt soft and comforting. "Pete gets these fits of rage sometimes, but they pass. It's related to his PTSD."

Heavy footsteps rang down the spiral staircase, and Kristy stepped back from him. His shoulder felt bare without her hand on it. Rob called out to Winston as he walked down.

"Oh, there you are. Have you solved our mystery yet?" He winked at Winston.

"It's pretty much cut and dried. The only snag in the day was being chewed out by Pete Russell."

Rob laughed. "That happens to the best of us. I guess you're ready to head home now to write up your official investigation."

"Which reminds me, do you have any written documentation on Joe? I should look over his record to be thorough."

Rob ran a hand through his snarled hair. "Of course, we do. There's a file on each of the residents. You can read it at your leisure in the break room. I'm going to get some dinner at the taco joint around the corner. Kristy, want me to bring anything back?"

"No, thanks," she said. "I'll eat my meal here."

"You're such a trooper," Rob said. "Winston, I advise you to take a break after skimming the file and get some food. I don't think you want to eat the dried-up chicken and mushy vegetables they give to the seniors."

Rob whistled the *Super Mario Brothers* theme song as he walked out the front door.

"I didn't know you guys served food here, Kristy. Don't tell me you cook it in the coffeepot?"

"Ha! No, we have it delivered. It's through the Meals on Wheels program. Have you heard of them?"

Winston shook his head.

"All across the nation, there are agencies that deliver meals to frail seniors in their homes or at centers. Actually, the entrees look pretty good, but I do have to cut items up or blend things on occasion for the residents. I don't really eat their food, of course, though Rob pretends otherwise. I bring a good ol' PB and J sandwich to work for dinners when I'm staying in."

"Staying in?"

"Yes. With a staff of two, somebody has to stay overnight with the residents. I usually take five nights in a row, and Rob takes the other two."

"That's a lot of commitment to your work. What about your home life?" Winston asked.

"I don't think my cat minds too much." He might just have a chance, with only a cat for competition. She switched her long braid from her left shoulder to her right. Didn't women play with their hair as a sign of sexual attraction? "Let me show you that file, Winston."

CHAPTER 6

KRISTY LED WINSTON to the large sideboard he had seen upon entering Sweet Breeze, the tabletop a previous repository for the residents' medications. Underneath the polished mahogany surface, two doors with handles were tethered by a combination lock. Despite the deft twist of her fingers, Winston spotted the code: 10-26-18. All those years spent watching pixels fly across computer screens had finally amounted to something.

The inner lair of the cabinet contained two shelves. The top one held pills. From the other shelf, Kristy extracted a thick three-ring binder labeled "Joseph Sawyer" and gave it to Winston. "Enjoy."

A blaring noise sounded from outside. "That's the meal delivery truck," she said. "The driver can never find an open spot, so he double-parks and pounds on his horn."

Kristy scuttled outside, and Winston retraced his steps to the nook of a coffee room. He opened the tome on the vinyl card table and skimmed through its papers. They all pointed to a frail ninety-year-old man, compliant with all authorities until his natural death in bed.

Case closed, I guess. Winston turned back to the cover page. Something nagged at him. What was it that Pete Russell had said? Everybody has their secrets? Winston's eyes narrowed at the emergency contact listed on the first sheet. Name: Jacqueline Harrison. Relationship: Ex-wife. Why would a woman leave a saint?

He entered the digits into his cell phone. Nobody picked up. Winston noticed another entry, in pen, annotated next to the typed information. It read, "Jacqueline's Daughter: Emma Harrison." Another phone number was listed. He bet that the straight, precise handwriting with a hint of flourish was Kristy's.

He tried the second number, and it immediately connected. A strong voice belted out at him. "Emma here." Even the heavy wave of static didn't soften it.

"My name's Winston Wong. I'm working with the Sweet Breeze Residential Care Facility on a case. I wanted to speak with Mrs. Jacqueline Harrison, but I couldn't get ahold of her. Your name was listed next to hers in the file."

"Oh," Emma said. "You must want to talk to Mom about Joe." A sigh rolled down the line. "I'm not surprised you couldn't contact her. When Dad's out with his buddies playing golf, she doesn't answer the phone. The best thing to do is visit her in person."

Winston looked at the 408 area code and glanced at his watch. A visit seemed feasible to fit in before the sun set. Besides, he wanted to get the real scoop on the so-called saint. "Okay. What's the address?"

Emma gave him a street and number in Gilroy. It would take a good forty minutes to get there.

"I'll give Mom's neighbor, Tom, a call to let her know you're coming."

"Thanks."

"No problem. By the way, tell Kristy I said hello. She's a great gal."

"Yeah, I know."

They hung up, and Winston smiled to himself. He was right about the neat penmanship being Kristy's. He saw the nurse herself hurrying through the lobby carrying foil-wrapped trays. "I'm off to talk to Jacqueline Harrison," he said as she walked by. "I'll leave the file on the countertop. And Emma says hi."

"Oh, Emma? Such a devoted daughter," she said before she disappeared behind an ornate side door. Her head popped out again. "Have a fun visit and a good night, too. It'll be lights out here after mealtime, but I hope to see you tomorrow morning."

"You can count on it."

Kristy disappeared again with a twirl of her braid. Winston stepped outside, whistling. Looking at his unticketed parked Civic beside the expired meter, he smiled. *It must be my lucky day.*

Despite the traffic, Winston arrived in Gilroy faster than he'd anticipated. He pulled past the outlets, turned down some side streets, and found himself in front of Jacqueline Harrison's home. It was a box-like ranch house, identical to the other models down the lane, except for its yellow daffodil exterior. Pumpkin orange trim added to the home's brightness.

He rang the doorbell, hearing a faint civilized chirrup from inside. Nothing happened. Only when he pounded hard against the front door did Jacqueline appear. She opened the door dressed in a slim navy sweater and gray corduroy pants. She lurched toward him and said, "Well, hello there. You must be Winston Wong. My girl Emma called my neighbor about your visit. Oh, there's Tom now." She waved at the house across from her.

Winston turned to see a young muscled man, wearing only a white tank top, peer through his kitchen window. The neighbor nodded at them and raised something in his hand in greeting, which gave off a brief flash of silver. At this distance, Winston couldn't tell if it was a metallic cup or a gun. He waved back slowly and pinned an innocent look on his face.

"Come on in," Jacqueline said. Her round green eyes welcomed him. Her silver hair was held back by two black barrettes, an endearing girlish gesture.

As they entered her home, Jacqueline's back straightened. Winston realized that she was taller than he'd first thought. With her hunched posture in the doorway, they had been the same height, but following her, Winston saw that she was a good three inches taller, landing her around the five-foot-nine mark.

The inside of the house was painted various hues of yellow, from the sunlight burst in the kitchen to the dull vanilla in the living room. They settled in the second spot, on some floral-patterned couches.

"Can I fix you a cup of tea?" she asked.

His stomach murmured in appreciation. "Thank you. That's very kind." He was flattered that she played the hostess, even as he intruded on her privacy. She walked into the kitchen with sturdy steps, but her hands shook slightly when she carried the teapot in. Winston offered to pour and soon they each held a dainty porcelain cup of Earl Grey in their hands.

"I noticed that you're the emergency contact listed at Sweet Breeze," he said. He blew on his steaming beverage.

"That's right." Jacqueline nodded. "Joe didn't have any other family nearby."

"Nobody else?" Winston took the silver teaspoon and twirled it in his cup, even though he hadn't added sugar to the drink. "I'm under the impression that Joe was somewhat of a saint."

Jacqueline's eyes twinkled, lighting up their emerald color. "He was very wonderful, but still a man. He had his quirks, like everybody else."

"I understand that you stayed close to him despite the divorce."

"Like I said, Joe was great. He was very sweet."

"So what made you two split up?" He wanted the gritty incriminating details. Joe must have been the type of man to up and leave a woman he'd vowed to take care of 'til death do they part.

Jacqueline took a sip. "I asked him for a divorce."

"*You* did?" He had thought that Jacqueline would be the key to dismantling Joe's aura of perfection, but now…

"Honestly, it was because of the creature comforts." Jacqueline gestured to the room around her. "I wanted a nice ranch house with fancy furniture. I like my trinkets." She tapped her silver spoon against the delicate cup and saucer. "Joe couldn't give me that."

"He didn't make enough money?"

Jacqueline shrugged. "He was a high school teacher, so he made an adequate amount. I don't need to live like a princess after all. The problem was he didn't ever spend the money, and I was still a student pursuing my own teaching credential."

"You left because he didn't give you enough spending money?"

Jacqueline blushed. "That was just part of it. The twenty years difference in our age played a role, too. I think I respected Joe a lot and idolized him, barreling headfirst into the marriage, but it never felt like an equal relationship. I fell in love with a man closer to my own age, had an affair with him, got pregnant with Emma, and here we are."

Winston's head spun with the revelation. After all Joe had gone through, the man had stayed close friends with his ex? "You were the one to leave Joe," he said again, trying to wrap his mind around the facts.

"While pregnant with my lover's child. To get together with the man I had an affair with," Jacqueline said. "Yes, I was a cliché. I never claimed to be a saint myself."

She shook her head. "I should never have married Joe. I wasn't the best match for him. Maybe he was meant to be a bachelor."

"Why would you say that?"

"Joe lived the way he liked. I could never get him to change the spartan look of his apartment. He never spent any money, on himself or on me. He would teach with holes in his shirts and his socks, and he proposed with a dollar-store ring."

"Maybe he was saving up for something?"

"He was saving for the sake of saving. I think it had to do with his childhood, growing up during the Depression. He didn't trust the banks and used to put his money into his 'lucky' socks. He started squirreling away dimes and nickels into this extra large pair of socks as a child. Later on, he exchanged coins for bills. I saw him put neat folded piles of thousand dollar bills in there."

"That's an interesting habit." Winston finished his cup of tea. "Thank you so much for the pleasant company."

"It's always nice to have someone over. And you tell that nurse Kristy hello for me."

He blinked. "Your daughter said the same thing. Kristy's quite popular with your family, huh?"

She gave him a sweet smile. "That nurse went out of her way to meet me in person just because I was the emergency contact for Joe. She even met Emma in her off-time, since it's sometimes hard to get in touch with me. Kristy figured she should connect with both of us in person just in case."

Winston made his way out of the sunshine-painted house, mulling over Kristy's kindness. On his drive back home, his mind ran over the entire conversation with Joe's ex. He remembered Jacqueline's description of Joe's hoarding habits. Lucky socks, huh? What would the lifetime savings be worth of a ninety-year-old miser? If someone at Sweet Breeze had known about Joe's cash stash, there would have been a motive to get rid of him. Maybe this was turning out to be a real murder case after all.

CHAPTER 7

WINSTON RETURNED TO Sweet Breeze early the next morning. The opulent home was silent. No jazz music played from the piano, no footsteps shuffled down the hall. He searched for Kristy in the common areas, the lobby and the break room, to no avail. He went upstairs to the administrator's office and found the door wide open. Rob didn't even hide the computer game that he was playing. Space music blasted from the computer's speakers.

Rob glanced up. "Oh, it's you. Hold on a sec." He gave his mouse a couple of hard clicks. "There that should hold down the fort for a bit. Are you all done with the investigation?"

"No. In fact, I wanted to speak to some of the residents again."

"Ooh, tough luck," Rob said. "They're out for their monthly salon field trip. They walk over next door to get their hair trimmed at Hair Solutions. They'll probably be back in half an hour or so."

"Okay, I'll wait until they return."

"Sure," Rob said. "I think you'll be more comfortable downstairs in the cushy lobby, though." He looked ready to get his gaming groove back on.

"No doubt about it." Winston saw Rob's head swivel back to the computer screen for more *Space Domination* even before he'd finished speaking.

Winston traveled down the cherry staircase. Since all the residents were out, he figured he could search their rooms to his heart's content. He didn't know how legal it was to sneak around, but they would never even know. Thankfully, none of the doors had locks. First, he scrutinized all the name cards outside each room, and he entered the only space without a name attached to it. He figured the blank one had been Joseph Sawyer's last place of residence.

Joe's previous room mirrored Pete Russell's all-one-color decor, except that it was dressed in green. The faint musk of Old Spice stunk up the place. Joe's space, like Pete's, also contained spindly sitting chairs and an antique dresser. A dark emerald color bathed the walls, the floor-length heavy curtains, and the furniture's upholstery. The one glaring difference between the two rooms was the large Victorian bed occupying a center location. Its solid carved headboard presented pictures of flowering vines. The dark bedspread, in a deep blue and green plaid pattern, tried and failed to offset the feminine wooden decoration. The comforter lay with one corner flipped up, so Winston pulled it down and smoothed it out. With the tug, a small batch of tangled white hairs flew down to the floor. It looked like a cat's hairball. Winston decided against touching it. He saw the glimmer of white tufts in the sunlight and kicked the entire mess under the bed.

He headed over to the ancient vanity and checked the drawers beneath the gleaming mirror. The first few were empty, but the corner of the bottom one held a scrap of paper reading, "Boy." He wedged it out and slid the drawer open, revealing the contents inside: a ballpoint pen, several California postcards, and a pack of playing cards. He searched all around the room but couldn't find clothes of any kind. No socks for sure.

He left Joe's room and made searches of all the other residents' dwellings. He discovered a multitude of scarves in Anastasia's room amongst hordes of jewelry. In Eve's, he uncovered a dizzying array of oversized muumuus. One paisley monstrosity was flipped inside out, showing off a large inner pocket. In Jazzman's room, framed photos of him at the piano with the other residents hung on the walls. Vinyl discs covered the floor in mountainous heaps. In fact, they almost obscured an old coffee cup with the initial "J" and an old Coke bottle. He hoped the janitor would discover the trash soon, because he wasn't about to touch those grimy remains.

When he stopped into Pete's room, though, he found the man himself.

"What the hell are you doing in my room?"

Caught off guard, Winston revealed the truth. "I'm looking for Joe's 'lucky socks.'"

Pete laughed, a deep growl in his throat. "I'll say. The man sure was lucky. He got veteran status without any real work."

"What are you talking about?"

"I'm sure he didn't get any nightmares over at his military desk job." Pete motioned over to his bureau. "Enough chit chat. Time for solitaire. Grab those cards in there before you show yourself out."

As Winston pulled the top drawer open and took out the deck, he noticed an American flag lying inside. "You fold Old Glory the proper way, Mr. Russell. It's shaped in a neat triangular package."

Pete's eyes flicked over, and he gestured for the cards. "Guess you do have some appreciation for military details. I ran that flag up every morning and wrestled it down every night when I had my own home. I installed the pole myself in front of the house."

"You're very devoted to our country, Mr. Russell."

"You better believe it."

"Kristy mentioned you served in the Vietnam War."

He grunted.

"A lot of our vets didn't get the honor they deserved..."

Pete opened the deck and pulled the cards out in slow motion. "I don't know. Things don't always turn out the way you expect."

"That's the way life works."

"Don't you tell me about life—or death!" Pete flung a slew of cards at his head. Winston dodged, narrowly preventing injury by a thousand cuts. "I witnessed enough of both during the war. I wanted to do right when stationed in Cambodia. We thought we were helping folks out there, but..."

The tragic Khmer Rouge. "Mr. Russell. You did the best you could. You were just following orders, serving our great nation." Winston picked up the scattered cards, one by one. "Life sometimes deals a messy hand, but you can start fresh and play again." He handed the tidy stack to Pete.

"You know what? You're a real walking fortune cookie, Winston." He started to shuffle, then paused. "But that's all right. How about a game of Go Fish?"

Winston heard the front door of the facility open. "I'll take a rain check on that, Pete. I have to do some real fishing now."

CHAPTER 8

WINSTON SPED OUT into the lobby and seated himself in a beige microsuede armchair just as the residents entered Sweet Breeze.

Kristy flashed a smile at him. "It's good to see you again. How do you like their new looks?" The residents seemed pretty much the same. Even Kristy wore her signature braid, except her scrubs had changed from white to a light blue.

Everybody filed past him, except for Anastasia, who stopped to twirl before him. "It's a shame that hunky police officer wasn't at the salon today. He usually goes there around the same time. Not much of a talker, though. He just smiles at Kristy and looks at us with his wide blue eyes. You'll have to be my first admirer, Winston." She spun and gauzy brown wrappings swirled around her, making her appear much like a human mushroom. Her arm, covered by a twinkling bracelet, sparkled during the dance. She waited for his assessment, but he didn't know what to say about her unchanged hairstyle. He decided to compliment her on the glittering arm jewelry instead.

"Oh, this." She twisted it to catch the light. "A gift from Rob. Straight from India." She admired her bracelet some more. "I'll have you know, my charms work on any man around here." She sashayed away from him.

After Kristy had settled everyone else in their rooms, she reappeared before Winston. "How's the investigation going, Detective?" Her eyes held a glimmer of teasing. "Tell me about your visit with Jacqueline."

"It went really well. She even offered me English tea in a dainty cup." He paused. "Did you know their whole family adores you? They think it's really sweet the way you visited them to connect."

She blushed, and her cheeks lit up with a flattering glow. "Just doing my job."

"You go above and beyond your duty," he said. "Since you're so in touch with the residents here, I wondered if you could answer a question I have. Jacqueline mentioned that Joe used to have a pair of lucky socks. Did he keep them here?"

Kristy laughed. "Yeah, he kept a crazy-looking pair of fuzzy socks in his drawer. Never let anybody touch them. They were an enormous, rainbow-striped affair. He never wore them either. He would just look at them and sometimes touch their soft exterior."

"Did you see them this morning?"

She shook her head. "I retrieved just his cell phone to send back to Jacqueline—that was the only significant item he owned."

Right as she finished talking, the front door opened. A uniformed paratransit driver, his handicap-accessible van clearly marked behind him, ushered in a gaunt elderly man in a wheelchair. The old man's posture seemed sloped, tilted a little to the left. Winston didn't know that a human could look so much like a skeleton. Only his full head of glinting silver hair contradicted the bony image.

Kristy stepped forward and smiled at the patient. "Harold, it's so nice to meet you. I'm glad that Green Hopes Nursing Home released you to us. Welcome to Sweet Breeze."

She gestured to Winston. "By the way, this man's Winston Wong. He's a detective working on a case here. Winston, meet Harold Meekings."

Winston gave him a brief head nod. He didn't think the old man could endure a handshake in his condition. "Pleased to meet you."

Harold gurgled out an unintelligible response.

"I'll show you to your room," Kristy said. She dismissed the driver with a quick thanks and a wave. "Winston, want to keep me company?"

"Certainly." Winston rushed to open the door to Joe's previous abode, while Kristy maneuvered the wheelchair into the spacious room.

She eyed the Victorian bed with distaste and turned back to her patient. "I wanted a hospital bed instead of that ancient-looking thing for you, but your family insisted on keeping the 'normal' furniture."

Kristy pulled down the plaid comforter and laid Harold in the bed. She fussed with the blankets around the old man. "There, that should be more comfortable. Let me fetch you a snack."

She excused herself and returned with a long clear tube and a can of Ensure. "Ready?" Harold gave a wobbly nod. Kristy pulled up his crinkled polo shirt and inserted the tube into what appeared to be a plastic button in the man's stomach. Winston took a step backwards, and Kristy looked at him, saying, "This is a typical G-tube. I'll insert Harold's nutritional drink through it."

"Um, I'll just meet you outside when you're done, Kristy." Winston flashed a queasy smile at her and hurried out of the room. He took several gulps of crisp air to revive.

Kristy showed up during one of his oxygen refills. "Sorry, I didn't warn you. You get used to that stuff as a nurse."

"It's okay. That's what I get for following you into the trenches. What happened to Harold? Why can't he eat by himself?"

"He suffered a stroke five years ago. His whole left side was paralyzed. Since then, his health has deteriorated to the point where he can't even use his tongue to swallow foods. His family placed him in Green Hopes Nursing Home in a hospice program a month ago."

"Hospice? Isn't that for people who are dying?"

"Yes, they give palliative care and relieve the pain of those with terminal illnesses."

"How come he transferred over here?"

Kristy shrugged. "Rob talked with the family, and they wanted Harold 'out of that horrible place.' They wanted a home-like environment for him when he passes away."

"Sweet Breeze is a nice place," Winston said. "And I hear the nurse is excellent."

She gave him a full smile, one that brightened her mocha eyes, and he drowned in their chocolate depths. A shrill beeping pierced the air and broke the moment.

"Your chastity belt, Princess Vespa?" Winston asked. He did a mental cringe.

"I think you've watched *Spaceballs* too many times," Kristy said. At least she got the reference. "That's the noise of the garbage truck coming down the road."

Garbage truck. Winston remembered that Kristy had stripped down Joe's bed after his death. Maybe some of those contents could provide a clue in this case. "Wait for me, Kristy. I'll be right back."

"Okay." She stayed still, a great feat for a much-needed nurse, while he sprinted outside.

The truck hovered two doors away from Sweet Breeze. Winston spied the large and bulging metal dumpster at the side of the house, hidden from the residents' view on the patio by a strategic hedge of bushes. He opened the lid with a heavy clang and looked at the contents. Flies darted out of the messy container. Remains of uneaten Meals on Wheels splattered the rusted metal interior. He spotted two neatly tied bags on top, no doubt courtesy of Kristy's prim handiwork.

He took them and peeped inside. One contained soiled adult diapers and used cleaning wipes. He held his breath and tossed it back. The other, equally noxious, held soaked bed sheets, blue plastic liners, and IV bags. He assumed Joe was the only resident who had needed his linens tossed out. He took the entire bag and locked it in the trunk of his Accord.

Winston ran back indoors, pleased to see Kristy still standing there. "Sorry about that. Where were we?"

She sniffed the air. "What's that smell?"

He must have acquired an *eau de garbage* from his trip. "I don't smell anything," he said.

"What's that brown blob on your shirt sleeve?"

Winston eyed the mysterious substance with disgust.

"Did you go dumpster diving?"

"I needed to get some evidence."

"Why don't you go ahead and finish what you need to do?"

Winston grimaced. He'd lost his tenuous connection with her. He stood there, uncertain of how to gain her back. Then he heard Rob's rough footsteps stomping down the stairs.

"Hey Kristy," Rob said. "Can you get that report on the new patient written up by six this evening?"

She faced him with her hands on her hips. "Right now? I have all night to write it up when everybody's sleeping."

"Don't you remember? I'm covering for you tonight. Once I get that report, you can bail." Rob rubbed his hands and winked at Winston. "I'm going to Comic-Con this weekend."

Winston understood Rob's love for comic books and knew that the trip to San Diego would be a dream outing. He gave the administrator a thumb's up.

Rob spoke to Kristy. "So I'll watch the chickadees tonight, and you can get them for the weekend. You're free to escape from Meals on Wheels tonight and get some real food."

"I need to take a break from investigating tonight, too," Winston said. "Want to join me for dinner, Kristy?" He held his breath.

She eyed the stain on his shirt again. "I don't know...."

"I'll pay," he said.

"Okay, just this once but only because I'm too tired to cook."

"Great, I'll meet you back here at six."

CHAPTER 9

WINSTON DUMPED THE contents of the trash bag he'd scavenged from the dumpster onto his office floor. Work before pleasure, he thought. At least the home's beige carpeting (now weathered to a dull gray with blotches of unknown origin by his bachelor ways) wouldn't be affected.

The immediate reek of decay grabbed his throat and choked him. There were wet bed sheets swathed in the acrid tang of vomit, bright blue plastic liners sprinkled with wetness—not urine, thankfully—and two clear IV bags with jagged rips in their plastic casings.

He knew enough not to touch the evidence outright with bare hands, but he hadn't remembered to purchase any professional gloves when he opened up his detective business. He scurried to his backyard and found a pair of unused gardening gloves from his dusty tool shed.

He was concerned about the gaping tears in the IV bags and wanted to know what had caused those gashes. The raging slashes could have come from one of Pete Russell's attacking PTSD mood swings. Plus, the man kept a stiletto knife in his room. What Winston required, though, was concrete evidence, not hunches. He needed to do some fingerprint testing. With care, he lined up all the incriminating materials in a straight row on his carpet.

Since the only thing he knew about fingerprint testing came from the *Phoenix Wright* game series on the Nintendo DS, he Googled the information. Thanks to the Internet, he scrounged around in his kitchen and resurfaced with starch powder, a match, and a basting brush. Following the directions on the computer screen, he lit the match and heated up one of his chipped pea-green porcelain dinner plates. A black film formed on the plate, which he scraped off. After gathering an equal amount of soot to starch ratio, he mixed the two together. He used the brush to place the homemade powder on all the items of evidence. He brushed and blew, waiting for dark telltale swirls to appear. The work was grueling; it reminded him of the experience spent grinding in a video game, trying to level up his avatar. He must have tried twenty times before he got any semblance of fingerprints. Finally, he wiped his sweaty brow and reached for a roll of clear tape from his desk to lift the prints.

He placed each image on a clean, white sheet of paper. Unfortunately, the smudges looked more like Rorschach blots than anything else. He could only find prints on the IV bags; the wet sheets and liners were useless for evidence. There seemed to be two sets of prints on the bags, and one set was smaller than the other. He wasn't sure how to distinguish them beyond that. Winston sighed and glanced at the wall clock, measuring how long it had taken him to arrive at a dead-end. It was 5:30 p.m.

Wait a minute. He needed to pick up Kristy at six. Winston ran into the bathroom and splashed his face with water. He used the lingering drops on his palms to tame the salt and pepper strands that stuck up on his head. He rubbed one hand over the slight stubble on his chin. He hadn't taken the time to shave this morning, so he pulled out a straight razor, added the cream, and went to town. For aftershave, he splashed on something called

Macho, and hoped the label would prove accurate. A tad more deodorant, and his personal hygiene was done.

He pulled on a pair of jeans without holes in the knees and a dark black polo shirt, the only dressy wear in his closet. He zoomed back to Sweet Breeze and arrived on the doorstep five minutes past six. He found Kristy in the main lobby, with her back to him.

Her raven braid hung down her back as her fingers swept over the piano. A slow rendition of a vaguely familiar tune traveled to his ears, and he started tapping his feet to the beat.

"You play wonderfully," Winston said.

Kristy's hands froze above the piano keys. She whipped her head around. "I didn't hear you come in."

Then her fingers massaged the ivory pieces again with light strokes. "Jazzman's been teaching me a little. I'm very much a beginner, as you can see."

The teasing notes caused a clear image to appear in his head, a shark with gleaming white teeth. "Are you playing 'Mack the Knife'?"

She shrugged. "I wanted to start with a song I knew already. What about you? Can you play an instrument?"

"No, I defy the Asian stereotype." He hid his stubby, useless fingers behind his back. "On the other hand, my sister Marcy quadrupled my aptitude, so I suppose that makes up for it. She plays the piano, the clarinet, the violin, and the Chinese harp." Marcy always teased him that his ineptitude came from Mom being pregnant with him during her cannery work, but Winston knew better. He would never be man enough to equal his sister's numerous talents.

Kristy's voice brought him back to the present. "Hmm, I wonder if your compliment holds any weight then."

"I can't play well, but I'm an excellent listener and judge of talent."

She smiled at him. "In that case, thank you very much."

Kristy stood up and faced him. He noticed then that she'd changed out of her blue scrubs. In their place, she wore a black scoop-neck tee with dark denim jeans. The curve of the shirt's collar, the slight exposure of bare skin, along with the glitter of her necklace drew his eyes to her body. He followed its lines down to her kitten heels, realizing how her everyday uniform didn't do justice to her figure.

Kristy cleared her throat. "Are you ready to go?"

"Definitely." Winston led the way out to his car and opened the passenger side of the Accord for her.

CHAPTER 10

AS THEY DROVE to the restaurant, Winston saw Kristy unbraiding her hair. The resulting tousled dark waves softened up her triangular face.

"Sorry," she said. "I forgot about rearranging my hair before you arrived."

"Looks good. It's nice to see your hair loose." He ran a finger down one silky strand after he'd parked in the lot.

"A girl's got to let her hair down sometimes," Kristy said. "It's been a while since someone's taken me out."

They walked together, not holding hands, but close enough for him to feel a potential surge of electricity if they did touch. Winston had chosen a chain steakhouse restaurant, a bit more upscale than Outback. He would've taken her to someplace fancier, but his budget didn't include wining and dining these days.

They found a table for two in the corner. A tealight resting on a tiny candleholder filled with miniature marbles cast a warm glow on their faces.

"How did your evidence digging go?" Kristy asked.

"I uncovered my first sets of fingerprints."

"Ooh, just like on TV." Her eyes widened. "You know, when I was little, I was a big fan of Nancy Drew."

"Thanks, I think. You're not saying that I remind you of a young girl, right?"

She locked eyes with him. "Not with your manly build."

He puffed out his chest. That Macho aftershave must be working full blast. "I was a fan of The Hardy Boys myself," he said. "And Encyclopedia Brown."

"I'd forgotten all about that brainy detective."

"That's why I call myself a 'sleuth,' in honor of one of his books."

She snapped her fingers. "That's right. Winston Wong, Senior Sleuth was printed on your card. You didn't want to write PI on it?"

He took two marbles from the centerpiece, rolling them in circles around his sweaty palm like mini Chinese stress balls. "You need to get hours of training and take an exam for that…which I didn't."

"So you're working under the table then?" She stopped his nervous marble cycles and placed the stones back. "Don't worry, I'm good at keeping secrets. I won't tell." He felt a weight of pressure leave him.

They ordered the three-course meal deal; he opted for prime rib while she chose the Porterhouse. He liked women who ate real food, not just salad at restaurants. Not that he had much experience. During his younger, not-so-bad-looking years, he'd suffered through a string of blind dates. The most disastrous one came from the personal ad his parents had placed in the local newspaper. He should have known trouble was heading his way when she showed up looking for "my side of sweet and sour."

Winston felt Kristy tap him on the shoulder. "Thinking about work?" She leaned close to him and lowered her voice. "What did you find out?"

It took him a moment to clear his head and respond. "Well, it's top secret—hidden even from me. I copied down some sloppy fingerprints that I need to match to suspects."

Her eyes sparkled. "You should have fingerprint testing on-site tomorrow. I think it'll make our residents' day. They often complain about it being boring at Sweet Breeze."

"That would make it easier to understand the clues," Winston said. "While we're talking about the case, I wondered if you noticed anything odd when you cleaned Joe's bed."

"Hmm, his bedsheets and Chux were wet."

"Chux?"

"Yes, those plastic blue liners we place on the bed to keep it from getting soiled."

"I noticed that as well. It wasn't urine, though. I checked. I think it had to do with the ripped IV bags."

"They were ripped? I was too busy bundling everything to notice."

"I hope to find out how they got torn tomorrow with the fingerprint testing."

"What else did you find?"

Winston ticked the items off on his fingers. "The IV bags, Chux, and bedsheets."

"Poor Joe." The sparkle of a tear slid down her cheek, and he rubbed it away. She looked even more beautiful in her melancholy. He wanted to keep his hand on her smooth cheek, but the waiter appeared bringing their food.

When the server left, Winston said, "You seem to feel a lot for your patients."

"Only natural."

"Because you're a nurse?"

"Not exactly...but let's eat before our food gets cold." She pointed at the juicy fare on their plates, and Winston's stomach grumbled in anticipation. He dove into his dinner. As they were chewing, there was a long stretch of silence, but he didn't mind. Hadn't he heard somewhere that if you were really comfortable with someone you didn't need to talk? Maybe he'd found a real potential girlfriend here.

Kristy finished off her dish but still didn't speak. Winston had to remind her about their previous topic of conversation. She sighed and tucked her hair behind her ears. "There's really not much to say. Basically, my grandparents raised me and my two younger brothers."

"What happened to your parents?"

Kristy lifted her fork and twirled it in the air. "They...weren't around, but Grampa and Granny were very hands-on." Kristy talked about her grandparents' unending dedication. They never failed to show up at recitals or sports practices, even when they were the only white-haired couple in the seats. She also spoke of her brothers; they fought a lot when they were younger. She, as the oldest, tried to boss them around more than they'd wanted. Now, although living in different states, they stayed in touch.

"Grampa and Granny passed on when I entered nursing school," Kristy said, "and I specialized in geriatric nursing in memory of them."

"How inspiring," Winston said.

Kristy pushed around the lingering crumbs on her plate. "Anybody else in my position would have done the same."

"No, I disagree. I think you're very unique."

She let out a tiny smile. "Enough about me. What's your background?"

"I grew up with both my parents, but they died of natural causes several years back. My sister Marcy is five years older than me and is the family genius. She went to Harvard for undergrad. Then she won a Marshall Scholarship and received free tuition to a university in England. She met her husband there and is currently one of the top herbologists in the world."

"Herbologist?"

"Yes, she studies herbs. It's quite specialized." He told her about all the speaking engagements and conferences his sister attended because of her expertise. He tried to remember all the scientific jargon Marcy had tried to drill in him, but he couldn't. Thankfully, he was saved when their desserts came.

Winston dug into his peach cobbler, while Kristy placed her crème brulée to the side. He let the fruity sweetness linger on his taste buds. "Peach cobbler always reminds me of my parents," he said.

"Did your mom bake a lot?"

He shook his head. "My mom didn't have time to bake. She worked seven days a week, with only fifteen-minute breaks every couple of hours."

Her jaw dropped. "What did she do?"

"She worked at CalPak, the California Packing Corporation. That was its original name, but it's better known by its second name, Del Monte. She canned fruit."

"Tough work."

"Yeah. She pretty much lost her hearing from all the zipping of the cans on the conveyor belts. She never complained, though. In fact, she called it a godsend, because she met my father through it."

"Did he work at the cannery?"

"No, he was in the orchards. He harvested peaches. The best way to pick up a peach, he always said, was to use the sides of your fingers rather than the tips to avoid dents in the flesh. One day, the normal delivery man couldn't make his rounds, so my dad volunteered to take the fruit to the plant. While there, he asked for a tour of the building, saw my mom, and fell in love at first sight. Peaches always remind me of love." He dipped his spoon into the cobbler and held it out to her. "Want to try?"

"Sure." She leaned over, pushed the spoon down, and pecked him on the lips.

Later, they ended up sharing the crème brulée using one spoon. Its sweetness didn't even begin to compare with her kiss.

CHAPTER 11

WINSTON DOUBLED UP on the Macho aftershave in the morning. He brought the necessary materials to the home (clean sheets of paper and an ink pad), but they were only props for his excursion. His real reason for visiting was to see Kristy again.

Everyone was gathered around the upright piano listening to Jazzman play, with the exception of the new resident Harold Meekings. Kristy stood bent over the keys watching Jazzman's fingers fly. Her hair was secured in its neat single braid once more, and she wore dull gray scrubs. Still, Winston could picture every curve of her figure beneath the loose uniform.

Applause jolted him out of his daydreaming. With the song over, Winston cleared his throat.

"Hi, folks. Hope you're all having a good morning. I need to get a copy of your fingerprints today for my investigation." He pulled out his materials and lined them up on the sideboard.

Nobody moved. Guess Kristy was wrong about fingerprinting being the highlight of their day. "Who's first?" He looked around the room, their emotions ranging from indifference on Eve's face to anger on Pete's. "Kristy, why don't you show everybody how it's done?"

She looked startled and moved with slow steps toward him. He didn't know why he'd called her name. She wasn't on the list. He just wanted to touch her again. He reached out and guided her fingers to the ink and onto the page. Despite their calloused appearance, the tips were smooth and velvet to his touch.

He called everyone up to the table one by one. Eve came docile as a dove, and her prints showed up crisp and clear. She brought the blackened fingertips to her eyes and grinned like a child who'd finished finger-painting a masterpiece. Kristy led her away with a gentle tug, probably to wash off the dark smudges already transferring onto her white muumuu.

Jazzman came next, his long pianist fingers rolling across the paper with grace. He hung around as Winston printed his name on the sheet in clear letters. "Would you like my autograph instead? I could still be famous, you know, and then you might want it framed up." He winked at Winston, grabbed the pen, and signed his name with a flourish.

Anastasia came next, with a slow waltz up to the sideboard. Her fingers felt clammy, and he had to do them twice because of the sweat marks. "Are you okay, Anastasia?"

"I feel odd doing this. Will you catch the culprit for sure?"

"I hope so."

After she finished, Anastasia walked away, wiping her hands in a slapping motion against her puffy black skirt.

Pete proved the most difficult to convince. Everyone had already gone back to his or her respective rooms, and the man sat there, refusing to budge from his seat on the couch. Winston had to walk over to the veteran to take his fingerprints.

"It's bad enough that I have to sit here for mandatory 'music appreciation' time," Pete said. "I don't need to be fingerprinted like a criminal, too."

"I'm just doing my job."

Pete snorted. "The only good thing about this is that I know you understand now that Joe was no saint. He must have messed up real bad to have someone go after him."

"So cooperate."

"Am I a suspect?"

"I want to rule out all the logical possibilities, like the residents here who have access to his room."

"I have nothing to hide."

"Quit stalling then," Winston said.

Pete folded his arms across his chest. "You have nothing on me."

"What about that stiletto knife you carry around? I found some slash marks on Joe's IV bags."

"Not lethal. Did you find any on his body?"

"His death was ruled natural, but I haven't seen the corpse."

Pete pulled out the knife from his jacket pocket and handed it over. "Take a look at this blade. I think it'll prove my innocence."

Winston saw that the blade was sheathed and dirt encrusted the entire holder, making it impossible to take out the knife and use it.

"This isn't a weapon," Pete said. "It's a sentimental item from my time in the Army. From the private who offered to check for mines in my place when I froze up. Two minutes later he stepped on one. All that remained of him was this knife. I keep it to remind me of his sacrifice. I could have died that day instead of him."

"I didn't know," Winston said. He almost placed a hand on Pete's shoulder for comfort, but he knew the man would shrug it off. Instead, Winston watched Pete hobble back to his room using his prostheses. Even without the new knife info, there was no way Pete could travel fast enough to have committed a crime.

Winston's previous number one lead in regards to the slashed IV bags had just walked away from him.

Winston decided to find some privacy as he continued organizing the fingerprints he'd gathered. He chose the break room, and it took him an hour with a magnifying glass to try and match the smudged markings, to no avail. At least he'd tried.

When Winston heard the shrill ring of a telephone nearby, he welcomed the distraction. A tiny cell phone perched behind the coffeemaker. Kristy must have left it on her coffee break. He counted five rings but didn't see her running in, so he picked it up. Maybe he could take a message for her. "Sweet Breeze, Winston speaking."

"Oh, Winston." The wispy voice seemed familiar. "Of course, Kristy must be busy as usual. Could you leave a message for me?"

"Of course, may I ask who's calling?"

"It's Jacqueline. Joe's ex."

He now recalled her dignified tones. "Thanks again for your hospitality. What would you like to tell Kristy?"

"We're having an open casket for the service. I wanted his friends and family to have a chance to see his face, say goodbye, and get closure, but the funeral home still can't stop the stink. Must be those new eco-friendly chemicals they use to preserve bodies." Jacqueline gave a nervous laugh. "I wondered if Kristy had some hospital-grade antiseptic."

"What kind of smell?" he asked.

"I think it's vomit. He must have thrown up on himself that last night, poor soul. They haven't been able to get the odor out."

"Poor guy," Winston said. "I'll give Kristy the message."

He jotted down Jacqueline's request. It must be difficult to spend your last minutes covered in your own throw-up. In that case, Winston was not looking forward to turning ninety. Wait, could it have been something else that had caused the vomiting?

He called up Jacqueline again. "Would it be okay for me to see the body?"

"Oh, do you think you can help with the odor?"

"I might be able to provide some assistance." And not just with the lingering smell.

CHAPTER 12

JACQUELINE INFORMED EVERGREEN Funeral Home of Winston's visit. She herself didn't accompany him. She couldn't be bothered to make the trip from Gilroy to San Jose. Besides, her daughter Emma, who was her typical driver on errands, was busy with her pharmacy work.

The funeral home looked especially drab compared to the splendid greenery that surrounded it. The dull gray squat building didn't even seem like a place of rest. It reminded Winston of the old packing plant his mother had worked in, slaving seven days a week in its concrete prison.

Winston shivered and walked in. At least the interior seemed more suited for serenity. The walls were painted an innocent natural beige, and haphazard Ikea nature pictures adorned their surfaces. Nobody appeared to notice him enter, but a door down the hallway was open. He could spy a tall figure moving back and forth in the narrow room. He called out as he approached.

A middle-aged blonde stopped her busy movements and extended a hand to him. "Oh, I didn't hear you. I'm Blaire the mortician." Her body held the grace of a dancer, and Winston could picture her as a model in her younger years.

He introduced himself. "I have an appointment to see Joe Sawyer's body. Jacqueline called about it."

Blaire wrinkled her nose. "The scent has been a problem. It's been days already. The smell should be gone by now. I already drained out his fluids and inserted the organic embalming fluid. I washed and dried his body for the second time today. Why don't you take a sniff and tell me what you think? My nose has adjusted to it and isn't as sensitive anymore."

She led him to a refrigerator against the back wall and pulled the large handle. It opened up to a view of Joseph Sawyer's naked body, laid out on a silver table. Winston flinched.

"Oh, would you like me to cover him up?"

"No, no. I just assumed he'd be clothed."

"I'll put on his formal attire once the smell has aired out."

Winston looked at Joe, the shriveled figure drowning in an expanse of metal. Filled with wrinkles, the man seemed a parody of a large prune. Winston focused on Joe's face, the source of his humanity. Lines crisscrossed it and spoke of numerous years, most of them filled with laughter. Joe deserved to have his death investigated, especially if it hadn't been a natural one.

He peered at Joe's skin. He noticed a figure-eight birthmark on the upper left arm. He peeked around folds and moved limbs. No cuts so far. He remembered Pete's claim about the useless knife, but he still wanted to make sure that no rough foul play had been involved. Then again, wouldn't somebody have noticed that? Or did people overlook suspicious causes in deaths of ninety-year-olds?

"Are you looking for something?" Blaire asked.

He placed Joe's leg gently back. "I was just admiring his skin."

She nodded. "He kept his body really well. Usually, I see a lot of marks. Older people bruise more easily. They get thinner skin as they age. With Joe, though, nothing."

No signs of unusual force then. Winston sniffed the body. "There does seem to be a rancid odor."

"It's not B.O.," Blaire said. "It's more of a sharp vomit smell."

As he took several deep breaths in, Winston started gagging. "Was it worse before?"

"Uh-huh. He must have vomited a lot. Maybe something he ate didn't agree with him. It takes a lot of throwing up to produce such a pervasive smell. It's almost like his body was reacting violently against something."

Maybe his food had been poisoned? He needed to check with Kristy when he got back. He covered his nose as another onslaught of stench assaulted him. "I did bring something for the odor. I'm not sure it'll work, though." He pulled out the spray bottle he'd been carrying. He used almost half the bottle of Stench Quencher, misting Joe with the stink-fighting drops. No dice. Something janky was going on, because if anything, the smell seemed to deepen and release a new odor.

"What scent did you use?" Blaire asked.

"It was fragrance-free."

"It doesn't smell fresh to me, but it seems sweeter now. I can't quite place my finger on it..."

But Winston could. It was the comforting smell of apples and cinnamon. And he'd remembered it floating in the air when he had first met Eve Solstice.

CHAPTER 13

WINSTON RETURNED TO Sweet Breeze and found Eve nestled on the back patio. She sat on one of the hard cement benches, her eyes fixed on the birdbath. She seemed to be waiting for birds to appear and drink up, but the water sat untouched, a layer of algae dusting its surface.

"Excuse me, Eve?" Winston asked.

The woman turned to him with a slow swivel. Her dull blue eyes seemed fixated on his chest.

"May I ask you a question about Joe Sawyer?"

A breeze ruffled the cotton candy pink muumuu she wore, but her body remained still. He wasn't sure if she'd even registered his question.

He tried again. "Were you near Joe when he died?"

Her eyes started wandering back to the empty birdbath.

"Joe, you remember him, right? You thought he was your husband... what was his name again? Teddy?"

Her head snapped up, and she fixed him with a sharp glance. "What's happened to Teddy?"

He twisted away from her ugly stare. "Uh, nothing. I have a question about Joe. Joe Sawyer."

"Don't lie to me. Tell me what's happened." She edged up closer to him and yanked the collar of his shirt. The top button popped off. "Family is everything to me."

He pried her dry fingers off his shirt one by one. "I'm the good guy here. I want to help you, Eve. Your granddaughter Carmen asked for my assistance, remember?"

At the mention of her granddaughter, Eve retreated and settled back down on the bench.

"I'm investigating Joe's death. Actually, I believe you called him Teddy."

"What? Teddy's dead?" She started wailing. The cries must have pierced through the glass doors, because Kristy stepped outside a minute later.

"It's okay, Eve." Kristy patted the old woman's back in a steady rhythm until her cries dwindled. "Why don't you rest for a bit? I need to speak with Winston alone."

Kristy pulled him to a bench several feet away. "Winston, you need to be gentle with her."

"You don't understand. Joe vomited a lot the day he died. Maybe somebody poisoned his food."

"His Meals on Wheels?" Kristy shook her head. "No, I monitor the distribution myself. Besides, everybody always eats the same meal."

"I smelled Eve's scent on his body. Apples."

Kristy massaged her forehead using quick circular motions. "Do you really suspect a woman with severe dementia? You're causing her unnecessary sorrow. Big chunks of her memory have disappeared, including the fact that her husband died. Every time someone mentions it again, she relives the pain." She pulled out a folded sheet from her scrubs pocket. "Here, let me show you something. This is the MMSE."

"Mini Mental State Examination," he read. "Which is?"

"It's a questionnaire to test your mind for signs of dementia. I was about to come out and evaluate her before she started screaming."

"Sorry about that."

"It's okay. I can give it to her some other day. I use the form every couple of months to record her cognitive status."

He scanned the sheet. Some were easy, like naming the date or year. "What's this one? Count backwards from one hundred by sevens?"

She shook her head. "I don't even know if I could answer that one. Most of the questions are pretty feasible, though. The test is scored out of thirty possible points. What do you think Eve got on her last exam?"

"I don't know. Fifteen?"

"She scored an eight. Dementia has taken a huge toll on her mind. She roams the hallways, aimless. Once, I found her fiddling with Joe's dialysis bag by accident while he was napping."

"That sounds dangerous." Maybe Eve had stopped Joe's medicine, even if not on purpose.

"I know what you're thinking, Winston, but she couldn't have worked out the mechanism in her state. Even if she had, it takes several weeks before the toxins build up to a dangerous level. I would have found out pretty quickly. I think she was trying to play with it like a toy that one time. Eve's harmless, so please be kind to her."

A sudden rich fragrance of artificial flowers wafted over to them. Kristy pinched her nose and looked toward the opening sliding glass doors. Carmen appeared, slinking her way toward her grandmother. She wore a lime green halter top, its V cut placed low, and shorts that rode high up her thighs. She held a computer tablet and hailed him with it. "Hey, Winston." Her lips cooed out his name. "Are you taking good care of Nana?"

Kristy's mouth compressed into a fine line, but she nodded a curt hello to Carmen before excusing herself to attend to the other residents inside the building.

Carmen looked at Kristy's retreating figure. "I wonder what's wrong with her. I saw her cover her nose. I hope it's not that second-hand smoke again. The administrator's always sneaking his smokes in the corner of the garden. Those fumes wreak havoc on my flawless skin." She leaned over Winston then, with her full bouquet of cleavage, before she settled down on the bench next to her grandmother. "Of course, you don't smoke, do you? Or drink? You're my kind of man."

How did she figure that? Did he look like a typical goodie-two-shoes Asian male? The fact that he hadn't smoked one cigarette or touched a drop of alcohol in his life didn't prove anything—she didn't know that. His sole addiction was to video games, starting with *Pong*. His parents had assumed it was a phase and that he would turn out to pursue the ideal medical or legal career path.

A gleam of flesh as Carmen crossed her legs interrupted his visual field, and he realized that he hadn't answered Carmen's question. "No, I don't smoke or drink."

"You took a little too long to answer, Winston." She wiggled a suggestive eyebrow at him. "Don't hedge if you have some fun once in awhile. I have my wild side, too. I let loose when I drink a couple of Cosmos. So now that we're better acquainted, why don't you come closer?" Carmen patted the spot next to her, her manicured fingers a gleaming moss green.

Winston sat a good foot away from her on the bench. "How often do you visit your grandmother?"

She slid closer to him until their legs touched. "I come by once a week, don't I, Nana?" She patted the old woman's shoulder beside her. "I'm required to," she said.

"How so?" He scooted away another inch, hanging onto the bare edge of the concrete.

"Well, I get this caregiver respite grant from a local nonprofit. They give me money to watch over Nana."

He cocked his eyebrow. "Doesn't Sweet Breeze take care of your grandmother?"

"Of course, but I provide her with emotional support and everything else she needs." She put down the tablet she was holding. He looked at the device's cover, which displayed a sketch of a woman wearing fig leaves holding up the Apple logo with her hand, a snake hissing above her head. Clever.

With her arms free, Carmen tried holding her grandmother's hand, maybe as evidence of the intimate bond she was compensated for. Eve's palm hung limp in her granddaughter's grasp. "Anyway, I need the money until I get discovered," Carmen said.

"Discovered?"

She struck a pose and pouted her lips. "As a model. I enter all the local contests, and one day someone will see my extreme talent. Then I'll be able to buy anything I want. I could buy a house like this one, a grand ol' Victorian. After that, I'll be a shoo-in for the movies."

"I see."

"How's the investigation going?" Carmen crossed her legs again, revealing even more skin if possible. "Do you need any more motivation to continue your search? I can help inspire you."

Her aggressive moves scared him. He couldn't help comparing Kristy's quiet beauty with Carmen's bold smuttiness. "That's quite all right." He stood up.

Her eyes narrowed at him. "Fine, then." She tossed her electric red mane and swiped her tablet hard, looking at the calendar that had popped up on the screen. "I'm off to a modeling audition, anyway."

His doubt about Eve hadn't panned out, but he remembered another suspicious find during his previous snooping session in the residents' rooms. He went to question the next person of interest on his list.

CHAPTER 14

WINSTON REMEMBERED THE coffee cup in Jazzman's room. It bore the initial "J," which could have meant Jazzman. But Basie was Jazzman's given name, and "J" could also stand for Joseph.

He found Jazzman cascading his fingers along the piano keys in the lobby. He paused at a juncture with a twist of his fingers and a grimace on his face. Then he continued again. That's right, Winston thought. Jazzman had mentioned his family tendency for arthritis. Could he have slipped Joe a fatal dose of his pain pills?

"Excuse me, Jazzman. I need to speak with you a moment."

"Mm-hmm." He finished with a flourish of the ivories and turned his attention to Winston.

"I want to talk to you about Joe's death."

"Yeah, I wanted to speak with you, too."

"Really?" Winston stared hard at Jazzman. Was the man ready to confess? He seemed as put-together as before, with his sleek silver vest and matching bow tie.

"I overheard something that morning, but it's so minor that I didn't mention it before. Except now that you've got us fingerprinting, you might need all the info you can get."

"Okay, what is it?"

"The morning of Joe's death, he squabbled with Pete. Nobody's on Pete's good side, but Joe got the brunt of it that day.

Kristy had set up this nice field trip to see a fine art museum, and she wanted everybody there. Like usual, Pete refused to go, but Joe decided to talk to him 'man to man' and convince him."

"How would that help? I thought Pete wasn't friends with anyone here."

"Well, the way Joe figured it, he would have the best chance with Pete, having been in the military. We all heard the ruckus, even with Pete's door closed. Joe was there for only several minutes before Pete started yelling at him and saying, 'You're no soldier!' There were some scuffling noises, but Joe came back out, unscathed. He seemed red-faced, though, and bothered by the argument. Pete didn't come on the trip."

"Did Joe seem scared afterward?"

"Nah, more annoyed than anything. By lunch, he was fine. He's not one to hold on to grudges. Not like Pete."

Pete would be a convenient scapegoat for Jazzman, and Pete didn't have a coffee cup with the dead man's initial in his room. Besides, Pete still had the harmless knife factor, and it didn't sound as if Joe had been too concerned about their fight. "I wasn't here to gather your observations about Joe's death," Winston said. "I saw something in your room that I want to talk to you about."

"You were in my room?"

"Just doing my job."

Jazzman nodded and scooted off the piano bench to sit on the microsuede couch. "Tell me what's going on."

At that moment Winston saw Anastasia exit her room, swathed in dark blue. As if attracted by the tension in the air, she edged toward the conversation.

Jazzman's eyes flicked toward her. "Go ahead, Anastasia. Why don't you join us? I got nothing to hide. Ask away, Mr. Detective."

Winston decided to hedge his bets. "I found Joe's coffee cup in your room." Jazzman colored and slid one hand across his close-shaven head. Winston had guessed right.

"Can you tell me why?" Winston asked.

"I always take several sips to prep before my playing. I find that coffee helps calm my nerves."

"I thought caffeine hypes you up."

Jazzman shrugged. "It works for me."

"He's telling the truth." Anastasia sidled in closer to the discussion. "I can vouch for Jazzman. He drank from Joe's cup every morning."

"Couldn't he get his own cup?" Winston asked.

"I can't." Jazzman placed his hands crisscrossed against his lap. "On account of my condition." He leaned toward Winston and whispered, "I have an enlarged prostate. Caffeine can cause irritation for me down there."

"You don't have to whisper, Jazzman," Anastasia said. "Everybody knows about your prostate problems."

"Shh!" Jazzman glanced around.

"Anyway, it's not an illegal substance, Jazzman. I heard on the news that coffee can even reduce your risk of prostate cancer. I, on the other hand," Anastasia placed a bejeweled hand across her chest, "can never have a drop of coffee again. Oh, how I miss a good cappuccino. It calls to my European blood."

She batted her shining eyes at Winston, extending the silence of her martyred pose. Winston decided to ask, both to be polite and to move the conversation along. "How come you can't drink coffee, Anastasia?"

"Oh, on account of my brain aneurysm."

"You have an aneurysm?"

"I know. That's why I fill my mind with all this information." She tapped one long jeweled finger against her temple. "You never know when it might go. In fact, coffee or any kind of stress might burst that blood vessel in my brain. So you just act real sweet to me, boys." She patted Winston's hand. "Anyway, I used to watch Jazzman sneak drinks of Joe's piping hot beverage all the time. Sometimes he would even steal Joe's entire cup and hide it in his room. Made me jealous, but I started to live vicariously though his sneaky gulps. You weren't fooling anyone, Jazzman."

"Are you positive that Jazzman drank the coffee the day Joe died?" Winston asked.

"Uh-huh. He did a startling rendition of my favorite song, 'So What,' right after the drink. Without the caffeine, he would have bumbling fingers. That's how come I'm so sure."

Hmm, then the poison couldn't have been in the coffee. Bricked—he'd run up against a wall, something that didn't work any longer, namely the method of poison distribution. At least according to Anastasia.

He wasn't about to trust his investigation on a lonely lady trying to endear herself to any man in her sight. Maybe she'd even made up the part about her favorite song to cover for Jazzman. Winston decided to investigate the sideboard himself. He knew that Kristy was diligent in handing out the pills and making sure the patients swallowed only their allotted share. He'd seen her meticulous work on the first day of his visit.

Winston slid over to the sideboard. Everybody had disappeared to their rooms, except for Anastasia and Jazzman who were deep in conversation on the couch. Perhaps all her frothy clothing would hide Winston's actions from their view. He spun the combination on the lock, 10-26-18, the numbers still engrained in his head from his observation of Kristy spinning the dial. He checked the top shelf, where every medication held a neatly typewritten label and instructions for usage. Jazzman received Flomax and aspirin.

It would be hard to gather a lot of his special medication, but what about the aspirin? Jazzman could complain about his arthritic fingers or fake a headache. Out of the kindness of her heart, Kristy might have given him a couple, and he could have stockpiled them. Or maybe he could have pretend-swallowed the pills. Winston shook the bottle. Unfortunately, the aspirin was almost all full, and the medication had just been filled last week.

How else could somebody have slipped Joe something fatal? The IV bags. Joe needed his special solution four times a day. Maybe somebody had tampered with the bags. That would explain the rip marks in them, because the perpetrator would want to cover his or her tracks. He remembered that the bags had retained two smudged sets of prints, which he hadn't matched during his fingerprinting analysis.

Winston decided to call the medical company that supplied the special solution for kidney dialysis. He extracted Joe's file from the bottom shelf of the sideboard. In five minutes, he'd found the company name. There was no contact information, though, so he climbed up the long staircase to enter Rob's office and search for a Rolodex. A+ Health Supplies appeared on the first index card, and Winston picked up the ancient rotary phone on the desk. He called the agency and secured a representative named Marlene.

Winston identified himself as a staff member of Sweet Breeze—it was pretty close to the truth. "I wanted to discuss a recent delivery," he said. "It would have been dialysis solution for our client, Joe Sawyer."

He heard the distant tapping of a keyboard. "I've pulled up your agency's account, Mr. Wong. I'm seeing a delivery that occurred three days ago." The exact day Joe had died. "A generic 2.5% dextrose solution, not the usual EXTRANEAL. Is this what you're referring to?"

It was all fancy doctor language to him. "That sounds about right."

"Frank delivered four 1.5 L bags of dialysis solution to your facility."

"Are you sure you delivered the correct solution?"

An edge of steel crept into Marlene's voice. "We don't make mistakes, sir. We have a rigid checks and balances system. An administrator oversees the supplies distribution, and it's double-checked upon leaving our building. We employ quality personnel here."

"Oh." It didn't seem probable that someone from A+ Health Supplies would have rigged the liquid. To achieve that goal would have required a high-level conspiracy. "I'm sure we received the correct shipment, Marlene."

"I thought so. Any other questions?"

"No, thank you." At least, he didn't have any more for her.

He needed some inside information. He spied a Post-It note on the tabletop with Rob's phone number: "Kristy, in case of emergency, my cell's 408-TOO-COOL."

He dialed Rob up.

"Kristy, is that you?" A flurry of noise rose up from the other end of the line.

"Sorry to disappoint, buddy. It's Winston."

"Winston, this better be good. You can't imagine the number of Cosplay cuties here."

He'd seen enough footage of "costume play" girls from his ex-coworkers to visualize some of the skimpier outfits they wore.

He'd better make this call seem important. "Rob, I'm thinking that Joe Sawyer may have been murdered."

"What? I think the crazy background noise is making me hear things."

"I think Joe's death wasn't accidental."

The noise retreated. Maybe Rob had moved to a quieter area of Comic-Con. "What makes you say that?"

"Well, it sounds like he'd been vomiting a lot when he died. I believe it was poison, and I think it was placed in his dialysis bags."

Rob let out a whistle. "Whoa, that's some heady stuff."

"I know. So let me ask you a question. First, what do you think about the A+ Health Supplies outfit?"

"Those guys are excellent. They're very reliable and reputable."

"Where do you keep the solution? I didn't see it in the sideboard."

"No, it's in a special medication cabinet."

"Who has access to that?"

An empty silence stretched down the line. "Well, you know that golden necklace Kristy wears around her neck?"

"What about it?"

"It holds the key to the cabinet."

"Does she ever take it off?"

"Not that I know of."

Winston cursed and slammed the earpiece down.

CHAPTER 15

WINSTON MARCHED DOWN the stairs, stomping on the polished ground, determined to locate Kristy. He couldn't believe that he'd gotten sidetracked by her attractiveness: the curve of her figure, the tangle of her loose raven locks. The first rule of a real detective was to not be swayed by a pretty face.

Halfway down the spiral staircase, he spotted Anastasia at the foot of the curve. She called up to him. "Are you okay?"

"Peachy."

"I heard some noises coming from upstairs."

"I've got it under control." He didn't want to shove an old lady aside, but if duty needed him to...

Anastasia started climbing up the stairs, huffing. "Sure you don't want to talk about it?"

If Winston had been in a better mood, he might have laughed at the sight of frail Anastasia, her skirt billowing out and swallowing up her body. She looked like a ghost floating up the polished wood. To hasten her ascent, he saw her lift her gauzy chiffon dress so she wouldn't tangle up her feet.

He decided he would go around her slight figure instead of barreling into her as he continued going downstairs. Before he stepped around her, though, his eyes caught a flash of color on her feet. He looked again. "Are you wearing fuzzy socks?"

The crazy rainbow-striped foot huggers clashed with the conservative dark blue fabric surrounding her.

Anastasia looked down at her feet, startled to see the socks' presence. "Oh. Those were a gift."

Winston's eyes narrowed. How many pairs of lucky socks existed in a senior home? "Perhaps from Joe?" he asked.

Anastasia stiffened and then groaned. "Yes. The man had no taste in hosiery. He wanted me to have a matching pair of socks."

"Can I see those?"

She gave him a puzzled look but pulled off the socks and handed them over. They were definitely fitted for a woman's feet. So not the same ones where Joe had stashed his life savings.

"What happened to his pair?"

"I'm not sure. They disappeared from the drawer they're usually in."

"And how do you know this?"

"Oh. Well, it's no big deal. Joe helped me out, all right? He would sometimes pull a few dollars out of those socks and, bless his soul, chip in toward my jewelry. I figured if there was any money left, maybe I could use it for a memorial gift."

"Several bucks? Couldn't have gone very far, what with all that pretty bling of yours."

Anastasia sighed and looked around to see if anyone was listening. "Look, I'm not a Russian heiress, despite what you may have heard. These jewels are fake. Most of my clothes I get from the thrift store." Her head drooped. "I'm actually an orphan and was adopted by a fisherman and a seamstress."

Winston felt bad pressing the issue further. He touched her bony shoulder. "Who knows, Anastasia? You don't know what kind of family background you came from. It might've been royalty."

She brightened up at his comment and caressed one of the glossy banisters before her. "Living in such a luxurious environment, I do feel like a princess."

"Yes, Sweet Breeze fits you."

"Thank goodness I got in before they changed the requirements. Now the residents need more than Medi-Medi and Social Security to be accepted in. Sweet Breeze requires a supplemental fee, either from a pension or family funds."

Anastasia had a lot of insight about the place, Winston thought. "Can you shed any light on Joe's death?" he asked. "I'm especially interested about the day he died. Did you see or hear him throwing up at all?"

"He was fine that morning. Shared the usual coffee and watched Jazzman work his magic on the piano." She wrinkled her brow. "I did hear a noise while taking my beauty rest. I sleep best during the early afternoon because all the night snoring disturbs me. Think princess and the pea."

"But you woke up that day?"

"Yes, I heard Joe talking in his sleep again. He said something like, 'Oh, it's you.' At first, I didn't think too much of it. I mean, we did have the mystery meatloaf for lunch. Later, he started coughing."

"Do you know when this occurred?"

"I'm not sure when he started mumbling, but the coughing happened right after two."

"How did you get that time?"

"I looked at the clock. I didn't want to miss bingo. I'm a pro at the game." She pointed at her large topaz ring. "I paid for this beauty with one of my winnings."

"Did Joe ever stop coughing?"

"No. In fact, it got worse. That's when I called for Kristy to check on him again."

"What do you mean, 'again'?"

"Well, Kristy always goes to Joe's room at one thirty to start his dialysis. He made those retching sounds for so long I got worried."

"Nobody else entered his room before Kristy checked on him the second time?"

"I didn't hear anybody except Kristy. You know, there's a creaking that comes from a loose board outside my room. Everybody squeaks it, although Kristy has the lightest step. It's only a faint whisper with her feet."

"I see, Anastasia." Winston squared his shoulders and gritted his teeth as he left.

CHAPTER 16

WINSTON STALKED DOWN every corridor of Sweet Breeze hunting for Kristy. In a twist of irony, he found her outside of Joe's old abode, now Harold Meekings's new quarters. She closed the door behind her and was stepping out into the hallway when he sprang upon her.

"When were you going to tell me about the IV bags, Kristy?"

"Winston!" She placed one strong but delicate hand against her chest. "You startled me."

"The bags, Kristy."

She looked at him, puzzled. "I'm not sure what you're talking about."

"Joe's IV bags."

"Do you mean his dialysis bags? What about them?"

"I told you they were torn before. Now I know why—because somebody was trying to get rid of incriminating evidence."

"They were intact when I hooked them to his catheter. They looked normal, no weird precipitate or anything. Clear as spring water."

"Oh, so I suppose you didn't notice the giant rips in them when you cleaned his mess up."

"I told you before that I didn't see anything." She counted to five under her breath. "You know, the dead body was the more noticeable item."

Her sarcasm didn't faze him. "Did you overlook the vomit, too?"

Kristy bit her lip, as if remembering the scene. "He did throw up, but I wrapped everything up in the Chux and tossed it out."

"How convenient." Winston pointed a finger at her. "It's easy to overlook the evidence when you're covering up a crime, huh?"

She narrowed her eyes at him. "Are you accusing me of something?"

"I think you poisoned him, Kristy. You swapped out his special dialysis liquid for something more deadly. Then you ripped holes in the bags to spill out the poison. Cleaned it all up and tossed it in the trash, like the good little nurse you are."

"You can't be serious." Her deep brown eyes bored into him. "You seemed like a better judge of character. I even thought you liked me."

"That's why they say you shouldn't mix business with pleasure, Kristy. What kind of poison was it?"

She placed her hands on her hips. "Let's get this straight, Winston. I would never, ever hurt one of my patients."

He agreed. She wouldn't do it out of straight malice. "What if you were easing his suffering? Securing a better death for him?"

"No, Winston. I'm in this job because I like it, even with the pension and benefits disappearing. I'm in it because *life* holds meaning for me, not death. I would have given anything for one more day, one more minute with my parents." Her voice rang out strong in the enclosed space. "You remember when I told you my grandparents raised me all by themselves? It's because my folks got killed in a car accident. An anniversary road trip on historic Route 66 turned tragic when my dad fell asleep at the wheel and swerved into a semi-truck."

"You didn't tell me this before."

"It was our first date. What did you expect? And does it make a difference on how you view me? Am I suddenly more trustworthy because of my sad life story?"

Winston heard Harold coughing through the closed door. Kristy turned her head toward the rattling sound. "Even at the end of their lives, I'm invested in each resident. Sure, we need to keep the beds filled, but to me, people aren't numbers. So excuse me while I do my work. And you know what? Maybe it's a good time for you to leave." She slipped back into Harold's room without another word to him.

CHAPTER 17

WINSTON STORMED OUT of Sweet Breeze's front door. He didn't want to work near Kristy's huffy attitude. Besides, he had some loose ends to tie up.

He surveyed the evidence still lumped in a pile on his office floor. He wasn't touching the vomit sheets. He eyed the Chux; they still retained splotches of unidentified liquid. He tilted the liquid into a new contact lens case, the only sterile container available in his home. He hoped the drops would indicate the source of poison.

He laid the sample on his scarred table and dialed the number he always called for help. The eleven digits took a while to punch in, but she picked up on the first ring.

"Marcy, I have an important favor to ask of you."

"And hello to you, too, little brother," she said. "Thanks for asking how I'm doing."

"Sorry. I'm on a time-sensitive case."

"Ah, so you've been successful in following your long-time idol, Encyclopedia Brown."

Unlike your previous career. The words she'd surely left out. He'd sought his fortune in the digital world, much to his parents' wariness. They understood the raw earth and its produce, not blips on screens. Even at the time of their deaths, they still worried about his unstable job. They'd probably extracted a promise from

Marcy to take care of her little brother. Well, he could fend for himself. "Honest to goodness, Marcy. I'm working on a genuine homicide case."

"Really?" Marcy's voice shifted from easy teasing to seriousness. "What do you need?"

"I think the victim may have been poisoned. Since you're the smartest herbologist on the planet, I figured you could test the sample. Maybe I could overnight it by UPS?"

"No." Her sharp voice cut in. Marcy always had a leader's commanding tone. "You can't ship something without knowing what the content is, especially if it's toxic. You could endanger other people's lives. Let me think..." She made several clicks with her tongue. "I have a colleague in San Francisco. Ruisa teaches botany at the San Francisco College of Herbalism. She'll have access to a decent lab there. I'll call her up now and tell her to expect you in an hour. How's that?"

"Sounds good, Marcy. I owe you one."

"Mmm-hmm. I'll put it on your tab."

Winston took off in his Accord to find the college. Despite the word "San Francisco" in its name, the campus lay closer to Millbrae. He was glad to shorten the drive by a good thirty minutes. He went around the drivers headed to the nearby international airport and took local streets to get to his destination.

He double-checked the address when he arrived at a rusty brown building. It looked like nothing more than a dilapidated apartment complex. On its front door where a trusty doorman might have held reign decades ago, a hand-painted sign read, "San Francisco College of Herbalism."

Winston pushed the door open. He went to the sole elevator, where a directory indicated that Ms. Ruisa Taz's office lay on the third floor. He took the elevator, a cramped contraption with a grated gate, and it abandoned him in a musty hallway. No framed pictures altered the deserted feel. He found Room 302 and used the brass knocker to announce his presence. No answer. He discovered the door unlocked and twisted the handle open.

Despite the creaking protest of the door hinges, the woman inside didn't turn her head toward him. She was bent over a microscope, her hands gripping its base.

"Excuse me, Ruisa? I'm Winston Wong, Marcy's brother."

She turned around and spotted him. "Oh, sorry. I lost track of time. Did you have any trouble with the directions?"

The woman's hands moved up and down with her words, punctuating each syllable. She was a vision of '80s fashion, from the denim shirt to the jeans jacket and Jordache pants.

"I wasn't quite sure I located the right building in the beginning. It doesn't look like the typical university."

"We're on a tight budget here. Don't let looks deceive you, though." Ruisa paused here and ran a hand down her lion's mane of tangled hair. "We're one of the best schools in herbalism."

"I don't doubt it." But Winston wasn't sure how many schools did specialize in herbalism. It seemed like a rare subject to study.

"Marcy said you wanted me to look at a sample?" Ruisa asked. He offered her the contact lens case.

"Um, I wear glasses." She pointed to the thin gold frames perched on her nose.

"No, I put the liquid in here."

"Interesting choice of a container. It's no matter," Ruisa said, "I have a state of the art lab." She gestured around the room.

He took in the beakers and pipettes arranged in haphazard array on her work counter. At least, the Bunsen burner was turned off. "How long do you think it'll take to get a result?"

"Well, there are no guarantees." She rubbed her forehead. "I'm only familiar with natural toxins. If it's synthetic, you'll be out of luck. Do you know anything more about the substance?"

"It's clear and odorless." He thought back to Anastasia's observation. "It also takes effect pretty rapidly and produces extreme vomiting."

"That's something to start with. I'll call you if I find anything." She took down his cell phone number. "You know, I wouldn't do this for anyone except Marcy. She's a sweetheart, and she doesn't need any more stress in her life. If I can help out one little bit—"

"What do you mean?" Winston asked. He thought his sister handled everything so well.

"You can't live her kind of lifestyle without feeling some pressure. What with all the speaking engagements at international conferences on top of everything else…"

He raised his eyebrows, but she refused to elaborate.

"Anyway, tell her to take the valerian plain."

He had no idea what Ruisa was talking about. "Uh, okay."

"I'll work on this all night long," she said and proceeded to turn her back on him and enter her private world again.

CHAPTER 18

WINSTON WRESTLED AT night with his dreams. An image of Kristy loomed large, her espresso eyes opened wide in hurt and disbelief. *I thought you were a better judge of character.* Her words rattled around in his brain.

As he bolted awake in the dim gray light, he realized he couldn't imagine Kristy as a killer. The conviction in her voice hadn't been rehearsed. Or perhaps he had fallen too hard for her, and he wanted to believe in her innocence. In any case, he decided to review the evidence again. He wasn't even sure Joe's death wasn't natural, but the extreme vomiting Joe had experienced seemed out of the norm.

When he drove to Sweet Breeze and didn't find Kristy in the main lobby, he sighed in relief. He couldn't face her anger this early in the morning. He headed for Joe Sawyer's old room, now occupied by Harold Meekings, for more answers. He didn't know how he would explain his snooping around to the old man, but it turned out he didn't have to—Harold was conked out under the soft bedspread. Winston looked around the dark room and spotted a slash of light on the carpeted floor. He moved toward the floor-length green curtains he'd noticed before but never investigated. Their enormous size hid a pair of glass doors that opened to the outside.

Winston stepped into the brilliant sunshine. Suddenly, he heard a shout. He peeked back through the door. Harold, with his eyes closed, was tossing and turning in bed. Sleep talking. Winston sighed in relief and examined his surroundings.

A hedge enclosed a small patio. No bistro chair or mosaic table could fit in the confined space. Still, it held enough room for a killer to hide while Kristy administered her duties, and for somebody to sneak back in and add poison to the dialysis bags after she was done with her work.

Kristy had claimed that the bags were unbroken when she'd started the dialysis. If she was telling the truth, somebody had to have come back to puncture them and destroy the evidence of their tampering. And since nobody had stepped down the hallway according to Anastasia's creaky step theory, that left only this spot as a means of entering and leaving. Winston looked around the hedge and found a break in the bush. He squeezed through the tight space and found himself in the back of the house. A pathway led right to the back patio. From there, anyone could have entered Joe's room after an innocent-looking stroll.

Something bothered him, though. The vomiting had occurred quickly after the dialysis started. That meant that the poison had been in the bag already. Who had access to the medicine beforehand?

A new answer occurred to him, and Winston headed back inside Sweet Breeze to investigate his hunch. Intent on his mission, he almost marched right past Kristy at the sideboard serving medicine to Eve. He circled back as he spied her red-rimmed eyes. The puffiness didn't serve her beautiful brown eyes well.

"I'm sorry I said those terrible things," Winston said.

She stopped filling the small paper cups with pills. In a weary voice, she said, "You sure seemed angry with me yesterday."

"I spoke without thinking. Now that I've had time to look at all the information, I realize I forgot a prime suspect."

She fiddled with the key on her neck. "And who would that be?"

"I think—"

Before he could finish, the residents began raising a ruckus about the slow medication dispensation. "I'll tell you later," Winston said. "And I'll make things up to you. I promise."

He hurried along the staircase and flung open the door to Rob's office. If anyone had a spare key to the medication cabinet, it was Rob Turner. Besides, wasn't Rob the first one to point the finger at Kristy? In fact, the locked glass medication cabinet lay in his room, next to a withered potted plant. The residents' medications were stored in cubbyholes, their names alphabetized along the shelves. Joe's name appeared in the lineup, but an empty space stretched above his label.

Winston rummaged through Rob's desk, disrupting official-looking papers, and found a key stuffed in the back recess of a drawer. He slid it out and tried it on the medication case; it fit like a glove. Now he knew for sure that Rob had access to the medicine beforehand. The question was: How to prove that Rob had intended to harm Joe? He needed evidence that Rob had known about the poison.

He looked over the documents on the desk again. They were boring papers on company regulations for claiming coverage for the residents. Some unopened mail lay on the side, too, with a tiny Swiss army knife on top. Apparently, Rob used the multipurpose tool to slit his letters. Winston flicked open the blade. A flicker of rust coated its sharp edge. This could have punctured the dialysis bags, he thought.

Winston searched the nearby filing cabinet. Rob's personal papers lay in there. Details about his salary (or lack thereof) plus his nixed pension and diminishing health insurance made Winston yawn.

He looked at the quiet computer and turned it on. Rob spent more than half his time with the machine. Perhaps his secrets resided there. It booted without a hitch, and Winston explored every file to no avail. In fact, at surface level, Rob seemed a conscientious worker. He even had an ongoing Excel spreadsheet to document his every task and justify his minutes at work. Winston wondered how much of the "reviewing resident files" time involved playing *Space Domination* instead.

Hmm, *Space Domination*. He typed in the game's main website for kicks. It featured zooming comets, grotesque aliens, and high-tech space stations. The log-in ID for "RobTurner" appeared on the screen. The password area remained blank, though. Winston wondered if he could crack the code. He wasn't a hacker, but he could give it a try. He entered "videogames." Rob wanted to get in the industry; maybe the phrase would work. No dice.

Winston scanned the room again, and his eyes landed on the framed comic book. Ah-ha. He put in "Eternals." No. Then he typed, "The Forgotten One," the name of Rob's favorite character from the series. He'd mentioned it when Winston had first shown up at Sweet Breeze. Nothing. Wait a minute. There was an alias for The Forgotten One. His fingers produced the name: Gilgamesh.

Rob's avatar showed up on the screen. In fact, it seemed similar to the comic rendering of The Forgotten One, the sleek version. Rob's character was dressed in a thick black space suit, his huge muscles defined under the form-fitting material.

A chat message popped up. "Hey R, ready to battle?" The sender's name was Zuras, another member of the Eternals.

Players of *Space Domination* could connect to one another via headsets and chat using their voices, but some preferred to save their breath.

"Sorry, not enough time right now," Winston typed in.

"I hear ya. How's old-farts land?"

"The same."

"Really? Did you try it?"

Try what? Winston wasn't sure how to respond.

"Let's go private," Zuras said.

All remarks in *Space Domination* could be read by other players. It helped people to make allies and coordinate battles. There was, however, an Easter Egg found on each level to create a private chat space. Winston searched the screen for the icon to click on; he remembered testing this scene before. His avatar stood on bumpy purple terrain, clumps of poisonous plants scattered across the landscape. Winston honed in on a plant with a tiny silver berry on it; all the others boasted attacking spores. His cursor hovered over the fruit. *Click.*

The toxic planet disappeared, replaced by the interior of a space capsule. Zuras appeared with his scruffy red beard, crammed into one side of the curved space. Sparkling stars could be seen through a tiny porthole.

"It's safe to talk here, R. Did you use the 5|_||cide 7r3e?"

Despite his confident tone, Zuras had used Leetspeak, probably as a precaution against snooping eyes. Suicide tree? Was he referring to the poison that had killed Joe? Maybe Winston could get some more information.

"I tried it," Winston typed.

"Did it work?"

"Quite well."

"Frag. One ninety-year-old fogey down. No more questions about your work at Sweet Breeze. No case for the ombudsman. And we get can rich from the geezer's stash. Don't forget we're splitting the cash fifty-fifty."

Winston's mouth gaped open.

"If you ever need more C3rb3r@ 0d0ll4m, I've got a great friend in India. It grows everywhere there." Something snagged at his brain. India. Anastasia had mentioned that country when she showed him her bracelet, which had been a gift from Rob. More connections to the administrator.

"Thanks. I've gotta go do some work now." Winston disconnected the chat and shut down the computer. He tapped his fingers against the polished desk. If only he knew for sure that Zuras had been referring to the poison that had killed Joe…

His phone beeped at him. On the other line, Ruisa's voice floated down to him. "I've got a match for you from your sample," she said. "It's a toxin derived from a plant that grows in salt swamps and marshes. The scientific name is *Cerbera odollam*." The name clicked in his head and translated into the symbols he'd just seen: C3rb3r@ 0d0ll4m. With his brain still processing the information, Winston didn't notice Rob until he'd already stepped into the room.

CHAPTER 19

WINSTON SCOOTED OVER to the visitor's side of
Rob's desk, trying to make his movements subtle.
"How was Comic-Con?"

Rob grinned, a smile as wide as the Cheshire Cat's. "Paradise. I
wish it had lasted longer. What's going on here? Are you done with
the case yet?"

"I still have a few loose ends to tie up."

"Do you mean that call you made to me about the dialysis
bags?" Rob turned on his computer as he spoke. The fluorescent
glare of the screen made his light straw hair seem white. The same
color as the tangled mass of white he'd found and kicked under the
bed when he'd inspected Joe's room. Winston felt his stomach
clenching. He was seated across from a murderer.

Winston shifted in his seat to look at the screen, to see if he'd
been found out hacking into the computer, but he couldn't see a
thing from his angle.

"Do you have any leads in regards to me?" Rob asked.

"Leads?" Winston could feel damp circles growing under the
armpits of his shirt.

"You know, any positions you could find in the gaming
industry."

"Oh." He gave Rob a small shake of his head.

"Didn't look, did ya?" Rob tapped a few keys on the keyboard and glanced at the screen. "No worries, though." He rummaged in the small refrigerator underneath his desk.

Winston could hear the pop of a bottle cap. Rob's head reappeared, along with two foam cups. "One for you, and one for me. Those bottles are a little too much for one person unless you spread it throughout the day, and then the fizz dies out. You mentioned before that you like Coke, right?"

Winston eyed the bubbling brew and licked his lips. He hadn't bothered to eat much of a breakfast before he showed up, and he couldn't pass on free soda. He'd raised the cup to his mouth when Kristy burst in.

"Excuse me, Rob. I need you to sign this form. It's for the new patient, Harold Meekings. I'm having issues getting some of the adaptive equipment through Medi-Cal." She set down her coffee cup and a load of papers on the desk. She riffled through the documents, picked out an ink-covered sheet, and dropped it in the administrator's hand. "I've documented his need for the item on the TAR form. Please sign here at the bottom."

Rob signed the paper with a rapid pen scratch. "Here you go, Kristy."

"Thanks. Sorry about the interruption, Rob." She turned to go, picking up her foam cup and the stack of documents. "See you later, Winston."

"Sure... I'll see you soon," Winston said. He was grateful she didn't hold a grudge against him. He watched the tidy sway of her hips as she walked away.

Rob cleared his throat, rose from his chair, and closed the door. "I see you're quite distracted by the nurse."

"Let me explain—"

Rob held his hands up. "No need. I'm flesh and blood myself. Remember, I met some cuties at Comic-Con, too." He winked and lifted his Coke up. "A toast to beautiful women everywhere."

Winston followed suit. The moment before the brew hit his lips, he smelled the stale coffee. Kristy must have taken his cup instead of hers. In deference to Rob and in need of something to fill his tummy, Winston decided to take a small sip of the warm liquid. Whether it was the fact that her lips had touched the foam or Kristy's special mix of coffee, he ended up downing the thing in several gulps.

"Good stuff, huh?" Rob steepled his fingers in front of him. "I take it Kristy's off your list then. Who's your new suspect?" He tapped the pen he'd signed the document with, a staccato beat that rang out in the small room.

"You."

Rob stopped drumming. His mouth dropped open. "What?"

"Don't play innocent, Rob. I logged into *Space Domination* and chatted with your friend Zuras. *Cerbera odollam*. Tell me about it."

"I don't know anything."

"Your friend called it the 'suicide tree.' Why'd you do it? Joe never hurt you."

Rob grew pale and shuffled some papers on his desk.

Winston pointed to the top sheet. "Maybe this is why. The way headquarters manages compensation for your work. Kristy mentioned that the pension was disappearing, and she told me that you guys get paid by quantity."

"Quantity? Oh, I see what you mean. Money is based on head count."

"That's right. So you murdered a man to get an increase in salary. When they keep cycling through fast, you get paid more, right?"

"That's preposterous. I would have to kill everybody in this facility to make money then."

"I also have another theory," Winston said. "Joe wanted to report you to the ombudsman. If an investigation occurred, it would have ended your charade of an administration job."

Rob crumpled the paper on his desk. "Do you really think I'm that coldhearted?"

"Yes, because there was the extra benefit of Joe's hidden cash." Winston saw Rob's eyes widen. "That's right. I know about Joe's savings. I also read his record. He had no family nearby except for an ex-wife who ditched him for somebody else. I bet you were thinking: Who would mind him dying a little early?" Winston narrowed his eyes. "You don't have the right to take somebody's life from them. I don't think the police will be very understanding."

"Where's your evidence, Winston?" Rob shook his head hard. "You've got nothing on me, just empty accusations."

Rob was right. Winston lacked true physical evidence. He needed the poison in his hand. He started ripping pieces off the empty foam cup in frustration. Then he froze. The Coke. It must have been tainted with suicide tree, an easy way for Rob to get rid of the poison tying him to the murder—and the detective asking all the nosy questions. Winston could already feel his throat tighten, and he put a hand on it in panic before logic settled in. He hadn't touched the poisoned Coke. Kristy had taken his cup by mistake. His eyes opened wide in horror. Kristy!

"You—you tried to poison me, Rob."

The office door burst open at that moment, and a uniformed police officer strode in. "Rob Turner, I need to take you in for questioning for the murder of Joseph Sawyer."

CHAPTER 20

THE BLOND-HAIRED POLICEMAN handcuffed Rob's hands behind his back. "I heard everything."

Rob glared at the cop. "What are you doing here?"

The officer jerked his thumb out the doorway. "A pretty nurse with braided brown hair saw me next door and hustled me over." He swept a few hairs from the back of his neck, strays from the clip he was receiving at the neighboring salon.

Kristy walked in, with careful steps, holding onto a full foam cup. "Here's the chemical evidence, Officer Gaffey."

Winston recognized the fizz of Coca-Cola from afar and breathed a sigh of relief. Smart woman. She hadn't touched the poisoned drink. Rejoicing in Kristy's well-being, he didn't see Rob drop his head and then suddenly swing it upwards with a growl. The movement clipped Winston on the chin. "You didn't give me any game leads, and you screwed up my current job."

Winston rubbed his aching jaw. "I told you it was hard to get into the game industry, especially since you didn't want to start at the bottom. Plus, you never liked this place anyway."

Rob tried to hurl himself at Winston, but Officer Gaffey stepped in. "I think I'll take him to the car now. Do you mind bringing the evidence out to me, Nurse Blake?" His blue eyes swept over Winston cradling his chin. "I didn't quite catch your name, sir."

Winston took a little bow. "Winston Wong, Senior Sleuth, at your service."

Kristy smiled while Officer Gaffey blinked at him. "Um, okay. Mr. Wong, unplug the computer and then make sure nobody else enters this room. I'll come right back for it. We might be able to copy or print out the chat conversation you initiated."

"It'll take me a couple minutes to disconnect everything," Winston said.

"I'll wait for you to settle Rob down and then come in a minute," Kristy said to the policeman. Officer Gaffey towed Rob away while Kristy stayed and watched Winston.

He moved around the desk to grab the computer and banged his ankle against Rob's mini fridge. He popped open the door and pulled out some ice to place on his hurt foot. While scrounging in the recesses of the ice box, he found a tiny vial marked "C3rb3r@ 0d0l14m."

Kristy peered over his shoulder. "More fine sleuthing, I see."

He smiled at her. "I could say the same of you. How did you figure it out?"

She shrugged. "Who else could it be? When you got so angry with me, I figured there must be some truth to your insistence on foul play. I never suspected any of the residents, but I thought Rob could be the culprit." She played with the golden chain around her neck. "I knew he kept an extra key around somewhere for emergency purposes."

"How did you know to swoop in and save me by swapping out the Coke?"

"An educated guess." She pointed to the incriminating vial. "Based on your poison in the dialysis bags theory, I figured he must have stored the poison on site. For sure, he wouldn't leave it at home for his parents to find, so the only place where he could have kept it was in his personal refrigerator."

She tapped at her temple. "Once you had the brains to figure out I wasn't involved, I knew you would follow Rob's trail. And when he realized that, he would try to poison you. No dialysis bags for you, which meant that Rob would try something else."

"Like poison in a cup?"

"The fastest way, and easy for him to transfer the contents over. These foam cups are all around Sweet Breeze, so I carried in my coffee with the 'important' document for him to sign on a hunch."

"You're brilliant, Kristy. Why did I ever let you get away?"

"That's the million-dollar question." While balancing the coffee cup with the tainted Coke, she reached for the vial with her free hand. "I'll hold that and you go unhook the computer."

"Yes, ma'am." He unplugged the various parts and placed them in a neat pile for the officer to collect.

"Well, with such polite words, I'm inclined to be lenient toward you."

Winston followed her sweet, undulating frame down the staircase. She grinned at him as he opened the front door for her. "I might be able to make some free time for you," Kristy said. "So you can redeem yourself."

He put on his best bright-eyed schoolboy face. "I'm all ears."

CHAPTER 21

SWEET BREEZE SEEMED to shut down in the few hours after Rob's arrest. A quiet air of shock pervaded the house. The residents stayed in their rooms with their doors closed. This was in direct contrast to Winston's own feelings. He was elated at the turn of events and had to hold back from banging on their doors and shouting about his awesome sleuthing powers. He wanted to yank each one out and give them high-fives. When he couldn't deal with their melancholy anymore, Winston left them to their emotions.

* * *

The next day he saw them all during a proper sad event, in the confines of the chapel at Evergreen Funeral Home. The small mourning party for Joe consisted of Kristy, all the Sweet Breeze residents (minus Harold Meekings, who was at the residential home watched over by a family member), and Joe's ex-wife plus her family.

An officiant stepped forward from the recesses of the room. He welcomed everybody to the funeral, inserted a generic commendation of Joe's soul, and then invited Jacqueline to give the eulogy. Joe's ex-wife, in a simple black sheath dress, stepped to the front of the small gathering. With her silver hair swept back, her green eyes glittered.

"Thank you all for coming. Joe didn't stand on formality, so it is out of respect for his wishes that this funeral service will be brief. Anyone who knew Joe remembers his sweetness. Not a bad word left his mouth. His perpetual goal was to bring a smile to everybody he interacted with on a daily basis. I want to recognize Joe for his contributions to this country and for his loving kindness to the people he met.

"I am very grateful for the chance to have been in a close relationship with him. He lived a long, full life. Although he suffered from kidney failure, he always exuded hope and happiness. I am comforted to know that his pain no longer exists and he is at rest. Thank you for being here and for your support."

Jacqueline hadn't mentioned any abnormality surrounding Joe's death. Winston wondered if the police had informed her about the arrest yet. He watched as she returned to her family, and they gathered her in a mini hug. Her husband had to be the older gentleman with owl spectacles. A constant wheezing contrasted his otherwise distinguished look and bearing. The middle-aged woman with auburn hair and the emerald eyes was probably the daughter, Emma. Jacqueline's own green eyes stayed on Winston's face as he surveyed the Harrison family, now complete and without the past hanging over them. Perhaps the death of Joe had meant a release for this family.

The officiant spoke again and invited the attendees to view the open casket and pay their respects. Winston edged up to the mahogany casket that held the man at the crux of his first investigation. On the soft satin cushion, Joe Sawyer rested. He seemed almost to be sleeping, and Winston's mind flashed back to his own mother's quiet death. She'd passed away in her bed, her face sweet and undemanding in her final hour (in sharp contrast to her actual personality).

Winston turned his attention to Joe's body again. The mortician Blaire had done a good job with the makeup. He seemed younger than ninety, with his arms crossed placidly and the few gray hairs on his head combed back. A previously white dress shirt—the color had mellowed to a buttery yellow over time—with an extensive array of ruffles hung loose on his slim body. Pinstriped pants covered him from the waist down. On closer inspection, Winston noticed they were made from a sweatpants-like material. He recalled Jazzman had mentioned that Joe was not "a snazzy dresser." Winston glanced back to locate the pianist and saw the man adorned in a black tuxedo, his top hat tucked under his arm.

After the viewing, the mourners walked/hobbled over to the verdant cemetery following the casket's dark sheen. At the gravesite, the officiant sang a hymn in a reedy voice. They lowered the coffin into the ground, and he prayed for peace over the departed and made the necessary soothing statements. Then people were invited to sprinkle a bit of dirt over the grave.

Jacqueline walked over first, her daughter trailing her by several paces. Jacqueline's husband stayed back. She placed an ornate wreath, an evergreen monstrosity, on the smooth wood. She sprinkled in a few grains of sand on top. Emma marched up. Her fingernails, painted a dark scarlet, seemed almost like talons as she dropped her dirt onto the coffin, accidentally scraping a sharp line into the burnished wood.

Kristy strode by next. She placed a large chunk of dirt in the yawning pit. She stood silent, peering down into the dark abyss and touched the gold chain around her neck. Her fingers rotated the chain like pseudo prayer beads. Winston stepped up next and placed a fist-sized mound in the hole. He paid silent homage to Joe and to his lost life. He thanked Joe for the beginnings of his detective agency and hoped that his unveiling of the truth had given Joe some peace in the afterlife.

When Winston stepped away from the grave, he saw the residents of Sweet Breeze lined up, each holding a memento in their hand. He wondered when they'd gotten the time to collude and scrape up an item for Joe's funeral. Maybe they'd planned it long ago, to honor their fellow friend together.

Eve advanced to the hole and placed a framed photograph on the dirt. The silver outline was tarnished and he could barely make out a face. Not a striking image of Joe. Winston imagined it must've been Eve's real dead husband, Teddy.

Anastasia moved toward the grave, and her voluminous black skirts dragged along the ground. He was almost afraid that she'd fall in due to the sheer weight of her fabric. From the folds of the enormous dress, she pulled forth matching cuff links (of sparkling cubic zirconia) and placed them on his coffin. She had probably used her costume jewelry fund to buy them.

Jazzman shuffled to the edge of the hole, his polished leather shoes glinting in the sun. He held a vinyl disc in his hand, one from his beloved collection from Sweet Breeze. He placed it on the growing pile of dirt and made a flourish with his top hat in a gesture of respect.

Pete acted as the tail of the troop. He stood ramrod straight before the grave. He wore his army fatigues under a faded black suit jacket for the occasion. From the pocket of his outer coat, he pulled out an American flag, still folded in the neat way Winston had seen from his room. Pete bent over and smoothed it down on top of the other items. He stood back up and gave a quick salute to his fellow veteran. Winston's hand almost rose up to his forehead, too, in response to the respectful gesture.

CHAPTER 22

THE SOLEMN PARTY all headed back to Sweet Breeze. Winston could hear a phone ringing as they entered the main room. The residents slumped onto the microsuede furniture, except for Jazzman who sat at the piano bench, his hands arched above the delicate keys without playing a single note.

Kristy ignored the shrill telephone and went first to check on Harold Meekings. She reappeared with a young woman about thirty years old, probably his granddaughter, who seemed relieved to be off-duty now. The woman bid Kristy goodbye and went out the front door.

The phone was still ringing off the hook. Kristy sighed and said, "I guess I should take care of that caller." She marched upstairs.

Ten minutes later, she came back down with a pale face. A stack of cardboard boxes shook in her trembling hands. "Listen up, everybody. I just got off the phone with management, and I have an announcement to make. Sweet Breeze is closing its doors." Anastasia gasped and appeared about to swoon, so Winston steadied her. The other residents sat stone-faced, except for Eve whose eyes wandered around the room in confusion. "I need to move everybody out by tonight. The owner thinks his reputation is sunk and is bailing out. He believes nobody will want their elderly relatives living in a home where someone's been murdered. He'll be selling the house, fully furnished, as soon as possible."

"Is that even legal?" Winston asked.

"No." Kristy scowled. "I argued with the owner about it. But he said he would send people to 'help us' vacate if I didn't comply." Winston bet the owner knew some shady Chinese Triad-type characters that could muscle the seniors out of Sweet Breeze.

Kristy passed out the packing supplies to each resident. "Everyone needs to pack up their items." She bent close to Eve. "Do you understand? You need to gather your stuff and put it in this box." The old woman made eye contact with Kristy and nodded.

"I'm making arrangements for all of you for a new place of residence. I'll do the best I can for you, and I'll handle all the transportation issues."

The residents scattered to their rooms, and Kristy started going back upstairs. Winston followed her and placed an arm around her shoulder. "Want some help?"

"No, you wouldn't even know where to begin." She sighed and moved his arm away. "Just go help the others pack."

* * *

Winston made his way downstairs, nervous about Kristy's slight brush-off. *Of course, she's busy with so many things, but can't she lean on me for once? After all, doesn't she realize I just solved an important case? I must have some skills.*

Eve wandered by him. "Where are you, Teddy?" She kept walking around in circles, moaning. "I've put your stuff in the box like you asked me to."

Winston stopped the old woman before she made herself dizzy. He took her hands in a gentle hold. "Eve, did you pack all your things?"

"But where's Teddy? He needs to come with me, and I can't find him."

Winston shook his head. "I'm sorry, but Joe—I mean Teddy—died. He won't be coming with you."

The woman's shoulders shook, and the items in her box clattered around. A ceramic mug jostled against some keys. "What do you mean he's dead? How did Teddy pass away?"

"Don't you remember the funeral?"

Her brow furrowed. "The brown coffin?"

"That's right. We buried Teddy today."

She wiped the sleeve of her oversized muumuu against her eyes. He could see the wetness of her tears seeping into the thin fabric. "I need to get my stuff then. I can't keep living here."

She took a step forward, then one step back. She squinted at Winston's face. "Who are you again? You're not the nice man that lives upstairs with us, are you?"

"Um, no."

"We rented a room to this young man. I want to tell him that I'm moving out. Where is he?"

Winston shuffled his feet. "Do you mean Rob?"

"Rob." She paused. "That sounds about right. Where's Rob?"

"The police arrested him."

"Whatever for?"

"For killing Joe."

"Who?"

"That is, Teddy."

"What?" Eve started wailing. Winston looked around for help as her screams escalated.

He saw Kristy run down the stairs. "What's wrong, Eve?" She held the old woman close to her chest, rocking her and making shushing noises. She threw a killer glare at Winston and said, "Some help you are."

He backed away. He needed to find someone else to assist and fast.

CHAPTER 23

WINSTON LOOKED FOR Anastasia in her room. Sweet Anastasia. Surely, she would give him no problems. Her floor was covered in a rainbow of see-through material, her discarded gauzy coverings. She wrapped him up in the folds of her flowing dress. "Winston, my hero. I'm so glad you uncovered Joe's killer. Poison through the dialysis bags, right?"

"Word sure spreads quickly around here."

Anastasia fluttered one bejeweled hand against her heart. "I wanted to double-check the facts. You were so thorough in your investigation, what with fingerprinting everyone. Too bad you didn't get a copy of Rob's prints then."

"Yeah. I remember you were very nervous during that session, Anastasia. I had to redo yours."

Anastasia's mood shifted. She hung her head, her pointed chin half-covered by fabric. "Actually, I was scared I was to blame for Joe's death."

"What do you mean?"

"The day Joe died, I was in his room. Right after Kristy left." So that's how Anastasia had really known when Joe had started coughing. She'd been awake the whole time. "I was furious at him. He hadn't paid enough attention to me on my special day. He even held that delirious Eve's hand instead of mine when they were singing 'Happy birthday' to me."

"So you went to confront him?"

"No, I wanted to get a quick birthday hug, that's all. I thought he would have stayed awake after Kristy did the dialysis, but the man was asleep, so I positioned his arms around me. He didn't wake up, but he started squirming. I didn't mean any harm, though I might have snagged his tube with my bracelets."

"Did it pull out?"

"I didn't think so at the time, but I didn't want to bother Kristy and have her check. It would have made me look like a fool, begging for a birthday hug. But I did call Kristy to come when I heard him coughing later on. Anyway, the dialysis bags must not have been disturbed since the poison was in them. They must have been in place for the toxin to enter his system."

"You should have told me this earlier, Anastasia, so that I could have all my facts straight."

"It worked out in the end without my saying anything, though."

He would forgive her this time. She hadn't meant any harm by withholding information. Winston started picking up sheer fabrics off the floor for her to pack.

Anastasia clapped her hands. "What a dear. Do you see my pearl wrap?" How could he even begin to search the fabric layers scattered around her bedroom?

"It's a white gauzy thing that I wrap around my shoulders when I get cold," Anastasia said.

Winston checked the pile in his hands.

"It's not in there," she said. "I already checked those. That's why they're on the floor. Oh well, never mind."

She took a wrap off the top of the pile, and something dropped out. Winston grabbed the white envelope with a ripped corner. "What's this, Anastasia?"

"Nothing. Give it back to me."

"This is addressed to Joe Sawyer." He looked closer at the torn edge. "I can't make out the return name, something Davies Law Offices."

She tried to grab at the letter with her birdlike fingers, but he dodged her efforts. "This is evidence, Anastasia. It could help us lock Rob away for even longer."

He pulled out a piece of paper from the ripped envelope. A letter on heavy parchment contained the header, "Boyle & Davies Law Offices." He skimmed over the legalese, deciphering it. "A cease and desist order from a lawyer named Tim Boyle. For Joe Sawyer to stop harassing Jacqueline Harrison?"

Anastasia wrung her hands, wrinkling the soft fabric she was holding. "Joe didn't have a mean bone in his body, so why would his ex-wife ask to stop communicating with him? It doesn't make sense."

"I don't know, Anastasia, but I'll need to keep this. Where did you find it?"

"It was in Joe's drawer." Winston then remembered the scrap of paper with the word "Boy" on it, presumably part of "Boyle & Davies Law Offices" stuck in its corner when he went snooping around Joe's room.

"How come you didn't tell me this before?"

"I didn't want to mar Joe's image with this absurd legal document."

"I see. You wanted to protect Joe's honor," he said.

"Thank you for understanding, Winston." She fixed her creased wrap and folded it into a tight square. "Now what was all that commotion I heard outside?"

Winston summarized how he'd alarmed Eve by blurting out the truth about Joe/Teddy dying.

"Pshaw. She's wired all wrong. Don't mind her bawling." She frowned at a wrinkle in the thin fabric she held and redid the folding. "Eve's crazy. Did you see what she brought to Joe's funeral?"

"A picture of her dead husband?" The image that hadn't matched Joe.

Anastasia snorted. "No, it was the original paper that gets stuck to a photo frame, the generic sample that says 5x7 on it."

"Well, she does have dementia."

"I know. She'll probably get to stay with her family because of her diagnosis, too. Although I don't know how they'll survive. Her wannabe model granddaughter can't even make enough money to support herself."

Anastasia plopped onto her bed. "On the other hand, poor me. Kristy will try her best, but I'll probably be stuck in a nursing home." She flung one arm across her eyes.

"It won't be so bad, Anastasia. I'll come and visit you."

She removed her arm. "You promise?"

"For sure."

"Okay then." She got off the bed and smoothed down the sheets.

Women, Winston thought. So dramatic. First Eve melting down, then Kristy lashing out at him, and now Anastasia flipping her moods like pancakes. It was time to find the men, the sane folks in the home. He backed out of her door as she started organizing her jewelry for packing.

CHAPTER 24

WINSTON KNOCKED ON Jazzman's door. The elegant gentleman's eyes lit up, and he gave Winston a warm congratulation for solving the case. Finally, a man after Winston's own heart. Someone who displayed simple appreciation for his skills.

Jazzman started placing bubble wrap around a vinyl disc. "Give me a piece of tape, would you?"

Winston pulled off a large piece of packing tape for him and watched Jazzman wrap the disc with tenderness. Jazzman patted the record once before he looked up at Winston. "I'm curious. What was the smoking gun that caught Rob?"

"It was a vial of poison the police discovered in his personal cooler."

"Really? What did it look like?" Winston described the container to Jazzman.

"That's odd," he said. "I didn't see that there when I looked at his stash last."

"When was that?"

"Well, on the day of Joe's death, I snuck into Rob's office to grab some caffeine. Remember, it was a big performance, it being Anastasia's birthday and all. Trust me, you don't want to disappoint that woman."

"But didn't you have caffeine from Joe's coffee?"

"Sure, but it doesn't hurt to double up."

"How did you get in without Rob knowing you were there?"

"Aw, Rob never comes in early. I just got there before he went into the office. I grabbed a bottle and hid it in my room." Winston recalled the used Coke bottle sitting next to the initialed coffee cup during his first inspection of Jazzman's room.

"Anyway, excellent work, Winston. I'm glad you caught him." Jazzman gave him a whack on the back. He placed his padded music treasure into his box and stared out into space. "It's nice that I can take my things with me to the new place, but I'm sure gonna miss the folks here. Plus, I won't be able to tickle those ivories anymore." He nodded his head toward the lobby.

"That's a shame. I enjoyed your playing. I know everybody will miss you, including me."

"Don't be a stranger then, Winston. Just ask Kristy where you can find me."

* * *

Since he was making the rounds, Winston stuck his head into Pete's room to check on his packing. "How's it going in there?"

The veteran grunted. "Don't have much stuff, and I'm used to moving around."

"Thanks for going to the funeral, Pete. I know you don't like walking around in your prostheses."

"I'll do it for an important occasion. I can't believe they let *him* go to the funeral."

"Who?"

"Mike Harrison." Jacqueline's husband.

"Well, he is sort of connected to Joe by marriage."

"Yeah, but he was the one who had ticked Joe off over the phone."

"When was this?"

Pete cleared his throat. "I haven't been honest with you. The day Joe died we had an argument." That's right. Jazzman had already told Winston this tidbit of news, but Winston wasn't about to reveal that to Pete.

"Everyone else was getting ready for the museum trip," Pete said, "and Joe had come in to see me and convince me to go when he got the call. He put his cell on speakerphone, and I remember the angry voice wheezing down the line." It sure sounded like the distinguished gentleman with breathing problems from the funeral. "Joe took pure abuse from him. Afterwards, I told Joe to man up, but he said that he'd been a soldier, too, and knew how to handle things. That's when I blew up."

So that's how the fight had started. "It's odd that Mike's still angry. Joe and Jacqueline's marriage dissolved long ago. I mean, Jacqueline did pick Mike after all."

"People don't have the proper perspective—they get caught up in trivial things—unless they've been in a war."

"Which reminds me. I thought that was a nice gesture at the funeral, Pete, honoring Joe with the flag."

For a moment, Pete's eyes seemed to search his bureau for the spot where his flag had been, but then they flashed back onto Winston. "I respect my country, and so did Joe. Not like some other people around here."

Pete paused in his packing and tapped at his prosthetic leg. "I sure didn't lose my limbs for schmucks like Rob Turner."

Winston nodded. "It was awful what he did to Joe."

"I knew he was trouble the moment I saw that bootlegged gizmo in his hand."

"Some sort of device?"

"Right. One of those initialed doohickeys kids like to play on nowadays. ES. GF."

Maybe the DS. Rob was probably sucked into *Mario Kart*, pitting his cars against others online. Winston knew plenty about that from firsthand experience.

"For goodness' sake. The man was supposed to be making his rounds during the night, checking to make sure we were safe, not playing games."

Winston scratched his chin. "Did you say that it was bootlegged? How could you tell?"

"Definitely a knock-off. It didn't even have English on the plastic frame, just funky swirls. Some kind of foreign language. I would have reported the man, but then he got arrested for murder. Even better." Pete smiled wide, the first grin Winston had ever seen on the man's face. "Now get out of here and let me finish packing."

Winston moved out of Pete's room and heard a resounding grunt from one of the doorways. He followed the sound to Harold Meekings's space. The noise sounded like a mutilated bullfrog call. Winston peeked in and saw Harold sitting up in bed. For once, Winston found it fortunate that his own dad had died of a massive heart attack, a quick and easy way to go. Harold, wasting away before Winston's very eyes, creeped him out.

Harold's eyes locked onto Winston, and his grunting grew stronger. The man bent his finger and crooked it, asking Winston to come in. Winston didn't want another repeat of the feeding tube experience, so he decided to find Kristy.

He located her in Rob's old office, about to place a call. She frowned at him and asked, "What do you want? Can't you see that I'm busy? I have to find homes for all my residents pronto."

"I'm sorry. I just wanted to—"

"Do you know what I have to do after that? That's right, after placing all these people, I'll need to find work. And do you know how I got into this mess?" She placed one quivering finger against his chest.

"Kristy, I was just doing my job. After all, I caught the killer."

"But what if people think I had something to do with the murder? Or didn't stop it fast enough? How does that make me look as a potential employee?"

Winston backed a step away. "I didn't know you'd be laid off."

"You're always looking out for number one."

She sure was stressed. "Wait, Kristy." He put his hands up. "I'm here because Harold needs something."

Her face softened. "What? Let me go find out what he needs." She placed the receiver back on the hook and tucked in the hair that had come undone from her braid. Then she marched out to find Harold without another word to Winston. It seemed like a good time for him to leave.

CHAPTER 25

A S WINSTON LEFT Sweet Breeze, he couldn't help but feel unsettled by the information he had received about the Harrison family. First, Anastasia had held onto a cease and desist letter against Jacqueline, and then Pete had talked about the argument between Joe and Mike. He decided to visit Jacqueline's home once more to get the story straight.

He took the freeway down to Gilroy. In front of the Harrison house, a classic buggy style car was parked in the driveway. He could see Mike Harrison tinkering away at its engine, a wrench in one hand. He would talk to the husband first to get his version of the fight. "Mr. Harrison, do you have a moment?"

"I don't know you, and I don't have anything to say to you." Mike straightened up and dangled the wrench in front of Winston's face. It glittered in the setting sun's rays. Winston wondered how it would feel to have the object "accidentally" drop on his head and gulped.

Mike peered at the house across the street, and Winston followed his gaze. In the border of the kitchen window, Tom the muscled neighbor held something shiny in his hand, too. Winston looked back and forth between the two men, debating where to turn, when Jacqueline's voice rang out in the twilight. "Mike, are you almost done out there?"

"Another ten minutes, honey."

Winston saw Jacqueline's figure silhouetted against the porch. "Is somebody with you, Mike? Oh, is that you, Winston? Come on in." Winston entered the Harrison home with speedy steps.

"What brings you to Gilroy?" Jacqueline asked as she settled a cup of Earl Grey before him.

Winston showed her the cease and desist order from the lawyer, and her face blanched. "I didn't ask for this. Mike must have requested it."

She put her face in her hands. "I shouldn't have used the checkbook, but I didn't want to mail the cash."

"You gave Joe money?"

"He would have never used his own savings. I wanted to help him pay for EXTRANEAL, the dialysis solution. Kristy told me his medicine changed to a more generic version about a month ago. In the clinical trials runs, EXTRANEAL works really well, and I'd rather Joe get a quality product."

"So you paid for the better solution?"

"Yes, and Mike must have found out."

"That's a really kind gesture, Jacqueline. So it sounds like Joe's insurance stopped paying, and you decided to help him out."

"It's a bit weird, really. I finally called the insurance company, and they said they still covered it, but Kristy told me the supply company only gave Sweet Breeze the generic solution. I'm not sure why it stopped." She fiddled with her tea cup, sloshing some of the liquid over its gold-rimmed edge. "Could you be a dear and check that out for me?"

* * *

Winston couldn't say no to Jacqueline's sweet face, so he found himself driving back to San Jose, hunting down A+ Health Supplies. He found the storefront from its neon lettering, a glaring beacon in the dusk. The building itself was about an eighth of the size of the giant drugstore chains he was used to. Winston almost had to hurdle over the wheelchairs near the entrance to make his way in. The pharmacy counter was located in the back, the better for customers to walk through aisles of medical equipment and snatch impulse items. Maybe a donut pillow to ease hemorrhoid pain? Or a leopard-spotted cane to show off around town?

He neared the pharmacist's counter and saw a tiny silver bell on the countertop. He felt like he was at a butcher's shop as he gave a sharp tap against the metal. A piercing ring split the air. A shuffling of feet, and a man popped out from around the corner. Instead of the customary white pharmacist shirt, he wore a ribbed tank top with jeans. "Sorry, the pharmacist will be right with you. She's in the ladies' room."

"Well, what's your name? Maybe you can help me."

"I don't give out meds." He straightened some pharmacy bags in the filing system behind the counter. "I'm Frank. I just keep things neat and tidy here."

Frank. The name flashed across his brain. "Do you make deliveries, too?"

"Yes, but I'm planning on becoming a bona fide pharmacist one day. Why?"

"Did you happen to deliver some supplies to Sweet Breeze this past week?"

Frank pulled out a clean cotton rag and started wiping fingerprint smudges off the counter. "I had nothing to do with that scandal."

"A+ is in the clear." Winston laid his business card on the now shiny tabletop. "Trust me, I'm in the loop. I just need more details about the dialysis solution delivered to Joe Sawyer."

"I haven't gotten my degree yet, man. I don't know about all that chemical stuff."

"That's okay. I know there was a change in the solution provided by your company. You guys switched from a brand name to a generic. Do you know why that happened?"

Frank shrugged. Winston could see the muscles rippling across his sleeveless shirt. "Sometimes families want to save money."

"I talked to the family, though. The ex-wife paid out of her own pocket to ensure that he received the brand name solution."

"Well, sometimes the doctor will prescribe both the brand name and a similar generic version. Maybe the physician wanted to help out his patient's finances."

"It's possible. Let me check that out."

Winston texted Kristy about the solution, receiving a message back a few moments later: "I remember the prescription. MD did not order generics. Jacqueline insisted on brand name. No more texts please. Preparing for interview."

Winston stared straight into the man's eyes. "Frank, the doctor didn't ask for generics. Is there anything else that could have occurred?"

Frank glanced around him and then lowered his voice. "You didn't hear this from me, okay? But our new pharmacist was very interested in Joe Sawyer."

"How do you know?"

"Her eyes lit up when she saw his name in the database."

"So you think she switched out the solution?"

"Beats me, but you can ask her yourself now."

Winston heard the swish of the white pharmacist robe before he saw Emma Harrison appear. "Emma, I didn't know you worked here."

"Part-time. It happened recently. They cut back my hours at the hospital, and I needed to supplement my income."

"It's funny to see you because your mom just sent me over here."

Emma raised an eyebrow at him and then turned to glare at Frank. "Get back to work. This conversation is none of your business." Frank hung his head and scurried to the back recesses of the pharmacy area.

"Emma, did you switch Joe's dialysis solution on purpose?"

She propped her hands out in front of her, elbows on the countertop, each palm like a scale. "Brand name. Generic. What's it matter? My mom didn't need to waste money on him."

"You didn't like Joe."

"Her old ex who was mooching off Dad's money? No, I didn't."

"Did Joe take money from your dad?"

"Not directly, but Mom always gave him stuff, including this brand-name solution."

"I think your mom meant it as a kind gesture."

Emma moved one palm way down, as if loaded by a heavy burden. "She does it out of guilt. If he didn't cheat my family out of money, he surely stole my mom's happiness."

"No wonder you looked so angry at Joe's funeral, scratching at his coffin."

Emma blushed a deep red, dark like her polished scarlet fingertips. "I know you're not supposed to talk ill of the dead, but that's the way I saw it. Joe was an emotional and financial burden on my family. I'm glad that he's gone now."

"Joe was murdered."

"I heard the rumors. The man was ninety. How much longer was he going to live, anyway?"

The front door whooshed open, and Winston heard a heavy gait tottering down the walkway toward the pharmacy.

"It looks like I have a customer coming. Is there anything else you wanted to say?"

"I think you should tell your mom about this."

She waved him off. "Maybe I will, maybe I won't."

Winston swapped places with the silver-haired gentleman approaching the pharmacy, the old man's quivering hand holding out a doctor's prescription. At the sight of the customer, Emma turned all smiles and cheerful greetings.

Winston wasn't sure what to make of the Harrison family, with the jealous dad and the vengeful daughter. He did owe an answer to Jacqueline, though, but he didn't want to give it to her in person. It sounded like that whole family needed to work out their psychological issues.

In place of a face-to-face conversation, Winston plucked a postcard from a spinning rack. One of those generic ones with "Welcome to California" in bold print featuring endless tanned bodies and spotless beaches as a backdrop, although he didn't even live near the ocean. He wrote a brief message to Jacqueline to talk to her daughter about the dialysis solution. He would stamp it and drop it off at the blue mailbox a block away from his home.

CHAPTER 26

WINSTON HAD JUST settled down to a late Salisbury steak dinner, courtesy of his microwave, when he got the call from Marcy.

"Hey, kid brother! Are you free this coming weekend?" A brief pause. "But why do I need to ask? You've got no social life."

"I take it you're not calling to give me a pep talk, Marcy."

"I can give you one in person."

"Are you headed back to the States?"

"There's a conference in your area. Do you mind if I stay at your place overnight? I get free housing at the hotel the next day, but I wanted to fly in a night early to get ready for my talk."

"You never stayed at my place before."

"Now that you own it free and clear, I'd like to see your permanent place."

"Yeah, thanks again for helping me buy it."

"What are big sisters for?"

"Guess what, Marcy? I cracked my case."

"Really?" She yawned.

"Gee, that excited, huh? Wait a minute, isn't it like four in the morning at your place now?"

"Couldn't sleep and wanted to get the details of my stay worked out."

"Gary doesn't mind your odd schedule?"

"We've been married for fifteen years. He better be used to my habits by now."

"Oh, okay. Well, I'll tell you all about the case when you come and visit me."

"That's fine. Pick me up at the San Jose airport. I'm arriving at four in the afternoon. I'll email you the details. Make sure you write it down on your calendar."

"Yeah, whatever." Marcy could be such a nag sometimes. It was a blessing she and Gary didn't have any children.

They hung up, and Winston stared at the phone for a moment. Despite having solved a big case, he felt like he'd returned to boring old bachelor mode. No date for the weekend, except one with his bossy big sis.

* * *

Winston decided to take a drive to see Sweet Breeze at night to revel in his victory once more. He parked and stepped out onto the sidewalk to view it up close. In the moonlight, the quiet house seemed eerie. A "For Sale" sign had sprouted on the lawn, the vampire stake at the bottom partially jutting out of the fresh, upturned earth. No crickets sang songs near the deserted home. He heard only the wind whipping around its walls, sounding like creaking footsteps.

He smelt a sharp scent on the wind. On the lawn, there were some joss sticks left burning in a ceramic urn filled with sand. No doubt left there by the superstitious owner. He'd be sure to want to appease Joe's angry ghost.

A flash of light appeared in one of the windows. Winston blinked and rubbed at his eyes. Another dazzle from a different room. He felt goose bumps rise up on his arm as he saw a ghost gliding through the rooms. It moved fast across the windows, the trail of pure whiteness an after image burning into his retina.

Winston shivered. With Joe's ghost haunting the place, how would they ever sell the building?

CHAPTER 27

THE NEWSPAPERS PRINTED scandalous updates: A big story revealed that Rob would be held in jail while he awaited trial. Another article divulged that people had seen lights flickering in the middle of the night at the old Sweet Breeze home and blamed it on Joe's bereaved spirit.

So when Winston passed the building a few days later, he was surprised to see a "Sold" sign planted on its tiny front lawn. After the ghost article, he'd checked the Web and saw that the asking price had dropped down by half. Even at such a low price, he wondered what kind of people would occupy a house filled with memories of death and disease.

His phone beeped at him. It was Kristy on his caller ID.

"It's so good to hear from you," Winston said. She hadn't kept in touch with him since the day of the arrest. He hoped she was immersed in her job search and not brushing him off on purpose.

"I have something important to tell you."

"What is it? Are you okay?"

"I'm fine, but I just got a call from Officer Gaffey," Kristy said.

"Gaffey…"

"The cop who arrested Rob. It turns out that there's a problem with the sample."

"Was it contaminated?" After all, it had been in one of those flimsy coffee cups and mixed with Coke to boot.

"No, there was no suicide tree in the batch."

"What do you mean? They couldn't extract it?"

"No, they didn't find any in the cup. Or in the vial from the fridge—they only found traces of water. Officer Gaffey says not to worry, though. Rob can be convicted based on the chat record and the physical presence of the vial in his office."

"There's still something odd about the suicide tree not being found." Winston hung up and drummed his fingers on the steering wheel. Had he been wrong? Could somebody else have murdered Joe?

He stared out into space and found his eyes refocusing on the Victorian house neighboring Sweet Breeze. Its sign read, "Boyle & Davies Law Offices." The letter. The Harrison family was a mess, but why had Jacqueline given Joe a cease and desist order? Was she truly unhappy behind the kind façade, as her daughter had suggested? Maybe she'd decided to take matters in her own hands by killing Joe when she didn't get legal results.

Good thing the hardworking lawyers were open. The Law Offices of Boyle & Davies took up the entire space of the beige Victorian home. Upon entering the front door, Winston found himself walking into a room that resembled a large library. Towering bookshelves with thick spines hemmed him in on all sides. The redheaded receptionist, barely twenty and model-thin, let him gape at the volumes accumulated in the main room before addressing him. "How can I help you?"

"I need to see Tim Boyle."

"Do you have an appointment?" She started tapping away at the sleek laptop on her desk. "What's your name?"

"I didn't schedule anything with him."

She blinked her gravity-defying long lashes at him. "Mr. Boyle can't help you then."

Winston pulled out the cease and desist order. "I've already received correspondence from him."

She seemed to recognize the company stationery. "Your name again?"

"Joe Sawyer."

The woman's deep blue eyes narrowed to slits. "You're kidding, right?"

He held his breath. Did she read the news or was she living in the typical self-focused youth bubble? "You don't look like a Sawyer," she said.

He resumed breathing. "I was adopted."

She hesitated for a moment. It was the pause of doubt, but Winston saw that political correctness won out in the end. She pressed the intercom button on her desk. "A Joe Sawyer is waiting to see you in the lobby, Mr. Boyle."

"Joe Sawyer? Now that I'd like to see. Send the man on up. I can spare fifteen minutes for curiosity's sake."

The receptionist told Winston to go up the staircase and turn right. He found the heavy oak door with gold lettering immediately. Tim's office was decorated all in brass. His desk edges as well as the handles of his clients' chairs showed off the same polished metal.

Both Winston and Tim stared at each other for a long moment. Winston saw a real-life Mr. Clean in a three-piece-suit looking him over through gold wire-rimmed glasses.

"I don't think you're Joseph Sawyer," Tim said. "You don't look like a dead ninety-year-old white male to me."

"No, Mr. Boyle. I'm Winston Wong." He handed the lawyer his business card. "I'm interested in learning more about this cease and desist order." He pulled out the letter and placed it on the desk.

Tim shook his head. "I don't understand why Joe Sawyer hired an investigator. It's a pretty cut and dry request. He needed to stop harassing my client's wife."

"What? Do you mean your client's Mike Harrison?"

"Of course." Mike, the man who'd argued with Joe on the cell phone. He did make more sense as a killer than his sweet wife.

"How, may I ask, does an old man bother his ex-wife when she's his emergency contact?"

"It's an issue of finances, Mr. Wong. Jacqueline used Mike's— excuse me, their—money to pay for unneeded medical supplies for Joe. Joe didn't have the right to demand that from her."

"Does it occur to you that she might have done it out of the goodness of her heart for a fragile old man?"

"That's not what Mike told me. He called it extortion. We're good buddies, so I told him I'd draft a cease and desist order to stop the nonsense."

"Well, it stopped—because Joe was murdered."

"I hope you're not suggesting anything, Mr. Wong. Don't you read the papers? They already have a suspect behind bars."

"There's some new evidence in the case." He decided to push Tim a little. "I wonder if Mike was the real killer. He was upset enough to ask for legal action after all. And he was overheard arguing with Joe the day the old man died."

"Don't level accusations at my client, Mr. Wong. Mike would never hurt anybody." Tim took out a brass ruler from his penholder and started tapping it against the rich wood of his desk. "Tell me, when did Joe die?"

"Last Tuesday."

Tim flipped through his calendar. "See, I knew it. We were playing golf then."

So Mike and Tim were good golfing buddies. That explained the quick and easy access to legal action on the part of Mike. "What's the name of the golf course?"

"The Pacific Golf."

Winston waited a beat, but Tim didn't even crack a smile. Where did people come up with these business names? "I'm going to check his alibi. If it doesn't pan out, at least I know Mike's got a lawyer on his side."

CHAPTER 28

WINSTON HEARD THE whir of the golf carts before he spotted the sign, the blue lettering disguised as waves: The Pacific Golf Course. He walked past the bronze gates and headed toward the all-glass building that looked very much like a greenhouse in the midst of all the rolling lawns. Behind the tinted azure blue panels, though, he could spy upright figures moving about. He entered through the automatic doors, which gave off a muffled whoosh as he stepped into a solid wall of air conditioning. Despite the severe chill, he saw people scurrying about wielding heavy golf bags.

He approached the front desk where a young freckle-faced blond man greeted him in a bored voice. "May I see your membership card, sir?"

Winston whipped out his business card and showed it to the youth.

"I don't understand, Mr. Wong."

"I need to check the company records to see if one of your regular members came here last week."

"We don't give out confidential member information."

Winston lowered his voice. "This involves a murder investigation."

The young man's head leaned in closer. Winston guessed he'd never experienced this level of excitement in all his quarter-century of existence. "Maybe I can help you just this once, sir."

"Good man." Winston gave him the date of Joe's death. "I'm checking to see if a Mike Harrison came in then and how long he stayed if he did."

The youth checked the computer system. "Yes, a Mr. Harrison showed up. He stayed from seven in the morning until five in the evening."

Winston frowned. It seemed like Mike did have a solid alibi. "Could somebody have impersonated him by using his membership card?"

"It's possible, but I don't think so. They'd have to be really close friends to swap cards." Tim and Mike were golfing buddies. Surely Mike could have handed Tim his pass while Mike snuck into Sweet Breeze to do his dirty deed.

"The computer shows that Mr. Harrison used his regular caddy on that day: Sam. He's probably on the field, but everyone has a cell phone for emergency purposes. Do you want me to call him?"

"That would be great."

Winston listened as the phone rang twice before Sam picked up. "It's Donnie," the young man said. "I have a private investigator here wanting information about one of your regulars." Winston didn't have the heart to correct Donnie about his proper title, Senior Sleuth. Let the boy raise Winston up in his esteem. "Did you see Mike Harrison come in last Tuesday?"

Sam's voice crackled down the line. "When doesn't that man show up? Yeah, he was here then, and the day before, and the day before that..."

"And you're sure it was him, right, Sam?"

"I'm not likely to be wrong about someone I've partnered with for over five years, am I?"

"Just checking. Thanks a lot, Sam."

"Later, Donnie."

Then Mike couldn't have been involved in the crime. He was just airing his jealousy and anger at an old man. You couldn't prosecute someone for that. On the flip side, though, it seemed like you could harass an old man with legal threats. The crazy justice system.

"Thanks for your help, Donnie." Winston handed a five-dollar bill to the young man for his assistance.

He went back to his car and fumed. Someone had swapped out the poison in Rob's vial. But who and why? Winston headed to jail to find some answers.

CHAPTER 29

ROB SEEMED DEFEATED, hunched into a ball behind the glass panel. He wasn't the same man who'd tried to attack Winston while being hauled off for questioning by the police. He had lost his spirit in the drab gray surroundings of jail.

Winston tapped the window and mimed picking up the phone. He'd just wasted hours of his day waiting in the jail lobby. And he'd been lucky—he should've registered ahead for a visit because of the mandatory paperwork. The staff had whizzed through the forms, though, and he'd been granted access after three hours.

Rob picked up his receiver piece.

"We need to talk," Winston said. "Something doesn't add up."

"I don't belong here. Jail's not for me. I used my one phone call to ask my parents for help, but they were so ashamed of me that they didn't post bail."

"You're lucky you're not Asian. My parents probably would have hung up on me and then disowned me. Maybe they would have even testified against me." What an extreme loss of face to have a criminal for a son. It's a good thing Winston had never gotten tangled up with the law. He'd only disappointed his folks with his odd computer hobby—even dropping out of college to pursue game testing—and his lack of girlfriends.

When Rob didn't crack a smile at his Asian joke, Winston said, "You know, I did find out something interesting today. They didn't find suicide tree in your vial." He wasn't sure if he could divulge this information, but he wanted to get Rob on his side, and quick.

Rob's eyes lit up. "Really? Great. Now you know I'm innocent."

"Okay, I'll bite. Tell me your side of the story."

"It was Zuras—"

"Your fellow gamer? The one I found in the private chat area?"

"Yeah, he suggested it. I was griping about my work. Venting. Then he talked about this toxin and joked about how easy it would be to get."

"It sounds like this guy just gave you a place to start. Malicious thinking is protected by freedom of speech."

"No, you don't understand, Winston. You need to detective the guy and hunt him down."

"Unfortunately, you were the one who had the labeled vial in your personal cooler, Rob. You must have ordered it. You've got to give me something to work with."

"I didn't buy the poison."

Winston sighed. "Don't play hardball with me." Rob wouldn't admit any guilt, though, so Winston decided to indulge a little more in Rob's fantasyland.

"How about you walk me step by step through the day of Joe's death?"

Rob took a deep breath. "That morning started off funny. When I went to my office, it didn't smell right."

"What do you mean?"

"I don't know. The air seemed disturbed. Anyway, I shrugged it off and went to Anastasia's birthday shindig. When I saw Joe drinking his coffee, I remembered my chat with Zuras, about the poison and all. I imagined Joe convulsing on the floor, and I realized that I could never poison another human." Rob shivered. "I excused myself early and went back upstairs. Later in the afternoon, Kristy came up to get some medical supplies. While there, she noticed something odd."

"Which was?"

"The door to the medication cabinet was unlocked. She asked me if I'd checked on the medicine. I told her I never touch her stuff. She laughed at herself, dismissing it as her own forgetfulness from when the medical supply company had last delivered a shipment. Then she left to attend to her duties."

"Did you believe Kristy had made a mistake?"

"Not really. Kristy always locks the medication cabinet after she's done with it. So I looked for my extra key in my drawer—and it felt warm to the touch."

Winston curled his fingers against the phone. "What did you do then?"

"I knew someone had tampered with the bags. Somehow I got the idea that Zuras had contaminated the dialysis solution. Call me paranoid, but I snatched up my Swiss Army knife. I didn't want to alarm any of the residents, so I snuck into Joe's room through a secret passage."

"Via the garden, entering through his outside alcove."

"You know about that?" Rob frowned. "I only discovered it since I smoke in that corner all the time."

Winston waved him on to continue talking.

"Kristy had already finished giving him the medicine. About fifteen minutes had passed since the dialysis treatment. I figured that wouldn't be enough time to get the poison pumping into his system. So I went in and cut the bags up with my trusty knife and waltzed out through the back." That explained the larger set of marks found on the dialysis bags when Winston had done his fingerprinting; they belonged to Rob. He assumed the smaller ones corresponded to Kristy's fingers. "After all, I didn't want to be caught wielding a knife in a resident's room," Rob said, "and I didn't want to be the murderer's next target either."

"Did Joe talk to you at all during that time?"

"No, he was out like a light." That was odd. Anastasia had mentioned Joe speaking to someone. *Oh, it's you,* he'd said. But if he'd seen Rob in his room, wouldn't he have been surprised by a rare visit from the administrator?

Winston's fingers cramped from his tight hold on the phone. He switched hands. "Did you notice Joe coughing at all?"

"Nope, he was sleeping like a baby."

"Interesting."

"Why? Did someone say otherwise?" A smile spread across Rob's face. "Is his sleeping soundly a hint that I'm not to blame? See, I didn't kill him." Rob puffed out his chest. "In fact, I'm a hero. I tried to rescue him."

Rob was right about the timing. According to Anastasia, Joe started his coughing spasm around two and keeled over soon after. Somebody else had been in the room after Rob, causing Joe's death.

CHAPTER 30

WINSTON CALLED KRISTY and asked if he could visit her. She invited him to her new place of employment at Life Circles. She explained that she did double duty at the two complexes on site, one for independent folks and the other for the elderly with severe limitations. She didn't mind the long hours, even on the weekends. She was glad anybody had hired her at all in light of the Sweet Breeze debacle.

He pulled into the asphalt parking lot that divided the two units and was immediately depressed by the view. One scraggly tree, bent far over in its concrete container, almost touched the faded blacktop.

The buildings on the left echoed the dismal parking scene. Their faded stucco exterior, bleached white from sun and wind, peeled in places. Closed windows dotted the walls, shuttered by thick steel bars.

The cluster of housing units on the right side, though, seemed a sharp contrast to the parking lot. Rows of gleaming townhouses glittered in the sunlight; each displayed a side lawn sprouting lush grass and bright flowers. Winston hoped to find Kristy in the second set of houses.

He headed toward the townhouse nearest him. Like the other cookie cutter models, it smelled of fresh paint. Brickwork decorated the lower wall, attempting to add an old school feel to the new building. The only difference between the office and the other units was the official-looking sign above the oak front door.

Winston walked into Life Circles' headquarters. A slender ponytailed girl, not more than twenty-two, greeted him. He wondered how the residents felt seeing her. Did they mind her youthfulness in their faces? Or did they pretend that she reflected them? Maybe if they were surrounded by young things, they would remain more active, too.

"Hi there," Winston said. "I'm looking for Kristy Blake."

"Can I tell her who's asking?"

"Um, a friend." Did one date count as boyfriend material? He'd been so long out of the game, he wasn't sure of the rules anymore.

"Another one? Popular girl."

"What do you mean?" Winston asked.

The girl shrugged her shoulders. "When she first came to interview here, that cute cop was with her."

"Cop?"

"Yeah, Mark Gaffey. Blond-haired, blue-eyed hunk?" The girl blushed and looked down at her short, bitten fingernails.

Winston tapped her on the shoulder, more of a sharp nudge than a gentle reminder. "So where can I find Kristy?"

She gestured with her thumb. "I think she's in the back room."

He went over there and found Kristy's head bent over a file folder. She twirled a pen across her fingers, deep in thought, and scribbled some more.

"Knock, knock. I can't believe you're working this late," he said. "Or maybe you're waiting for someone."

She gave him a puzzled look. "Yeah, you. I usually work these hours to catch up on my paperwork." She added the folder to a pile before her. "Out of twelve patients, I've only updated two charts. You're here about what Officer Gaffey said, right?"

"Speaking of Mark Gaffey, has he been visiting you lately?"

"No. Why would he?"

"The girl out front said she saw you two together when you showed up to interview."

"Oh, yes. Mark's great-aunt lives on the independent side. He told me Life Circles had an open position for a nurse and was kind enough to drop me off when he went to visit his great-aunt."

"Oh, it's Mark now, is it?" Winston could feel his lips tighten into a thin, flat line. "How very convenient that he found you a job."

She clucked her tongue at him. "Do I detect a hint of jealousy?"

He put his hands up in the air. "All I'm saying is the guy happens to visit the hair salon at the same time every month when you take the Sweet Breeze residents to get haircuts." He still remembered Anastasia's comment about the "hunky" policeman. "Then he sets up a job for you where he can watch your every move."

"He's a cop, Winston, not a stalker. What's really bugging you?"

Winston looked down at his feet and shuffled them. "Honestly? I like seeing you exclusively, Kristy. It's not all about the case for me, you know."

She nudged him with her pen until he focused on her. "There's nothing between Officer Gaffey and me," Kristy said. "And I'm sorry about lashing out at you before. It was really stressful arranging all the transfers and finding a job to boot."

"Then we can still see each other?"

"Yes, let's try again."

Heartened by her answer, Winston decided to do some boasting. "Now that you mentioned the case, though, I followed up on the vial discrepancy you mentioned and uncovered some new info."

"How?"

"I visited Rob in jail," Winston said.

The sound of the administrator's name made Kristy stiffen her shoulders. "How do you work with a man for two years and not know him at all?"

"If it makes you feel better, he's taking his new surroundings pretty hard. Plus, he's pinning the blame on his co-gamer, alias Zuras."

"He's transferring the crime onto someone he's never met before?" Kristy's pen flew out of her hand and into Winston's face.

He blocked it before it stabbed him in the eye and handed it back to her. "Rob said that Zuras was the one talking about poisoning Joe."

"Rob was still the one who did the deed, though."

"I don't know." Winston frowned. "According to Anastasia, Joe's coughing fits didn't start until shortly after two, a good amount of time after you'd started the dialysis."

"What if the suicide tree just didn't kick in until later?"

"That's a possibility, but if he'd stuck the poison in the bags, then why did he cut them up after the treatment began?"

Kristy's eyes grew wide. "He told you that?"

"Yeah, and I remember Anastasia mentioned hearing Joe talk before his vomiting fit. She thought he'd been sleep-talking, but now I'm not so sure. If he had a visitor, it wasn't Rob, who had already left by that time."

"Rob could have lied about the time he went into the room."

"I know, but Anastasia told me Joe said, 'Oh, it's you.' That means it's somebody he was familiar with—probably not Rob, since he spent most of his days upstairs in the office."

Kristy's brow furrowed. "Who do you think he spoke with?"

"I have no idea, but while I was driving today, I saw that the old Sweet Breeze house got sold. Do you think it's connected?"

"Unlikely. Folks will snatch up a good deal to live around here, even if the place is haunted." Kristy turned back to her mound of paperwork and started doing the pen acrobatics again.

"Don't stay working too long. It's getting really dark." Winston placed his palm on her shoulder. "Do you have time for lunch with me tomorrow?"

She squeezed his hand and gave him a brief smile. "Definitely, Sherlock. The Jukebox Café at noon. Don't be late from all your snooping."

"I won't." But the case was still a priority. Even though he had no new leads, he harbored a growing suspicion that Rob Turner had been framed. Unfortunately, Winston had played an inadvertent part in that, so now he felt responsible to root out the real killer.

CHAPTER 31

WINSTON PULLED UP to the old Sweet Breeze house, hoping to stumble onto more clues. He was surprised to see the changes that had been made in only one day. The "Sold" sign had been uprooted. The grass was smoothed over and gave off the appearance of an undisturbed, fluffy green lawn. A line of potted plants stood in the back, the geraniums exhibiting a rainbow of colors. A stylized sign replaced the Sweet Breeze name; drawn with vines and flowers, it proclaimed, "Home Sweet Home" in a florid script.

He pressed the doorbell and heard a metallic *ting* from inside. No footsteps approached. He pounded against the door, to no avail. He even pulled out his cell phone and placed a call to Sweet Breeze's old number. Of course, the line had been disconnected.

Winston glanced around at the traffic. All the drivers seemed intent on their errands or on their upcoming lunch. Nobody would notice the short Asian man sneaking up to the bay window of an old Victorian house. Thankfully, the new owner hadn't had time to change the drapery yet. The curtains remained the original flimsy lace kind. Though they were pulled closed, Winston could peek into one of the fabric's eyelets to get a look inside.

The microsuede couch and armchairs were gone, but the upright piano remained; a laptop perched on top of it, the computer screen open and emitting a soft glow. On the wall opposite the moved couch, Winston spotted a flat screen TV. Its expanse covered more than half of the white space. Somebody certainly knew how to live it up in their new home.

Winston moved back to the front door and tried to turn the handle. Of course, the new owners wouldn't have left it unlocked for him to waltz right in. He also checked the windows, none of which had been left open. He moved around to the back patio, where the sliding doors were bolted down tight. He thought he heard a noise coming from one of the rooms, a heavy thumping sound, so he ran back to the front. He stood a moment glaring at the locked house of secrets. Maybe Kristy would have a better idea on how to reenter her old work place.

* * *

The Jukebox Café was tucked away in one of the downtown side streets. Its name was announced in a garish neon sign that stayed lit from morning 'til evening. The interior smelled of fried grease and tasted of smoke. Whenever he ate at the place, Winston found layers of oil added to his hair. Still, it served filling diner fare for five dollars a plate, well within his detective budget. Plus, it held a cherry red jukebox that played oldies tunes. Its volume setting drowned out distracting ambient conversations, while not being loud enough to damage his eardrums.

He slid into the sticky booth where Kristy already sat peering at a menu. "Am I late? I was checking out a lead."

She glanced up. "No, I left a couple minutes early. I needed a break."

"Would an omelet cheer you up?"

"A free one might." She grinned at him, and he wanted to kiss the tiredness out of her eyes.

"You're working too hard at Life Circles."

"I could say the same about you and Joe's case. Maybe you're overthinking things. Rob's word shouldn't be trusted."

"I don't know. I have a funny feeling that he's telling the truth."

"Or maybe you should just pat yourself on the back, and let the justice system run its due course with Rob."

"I tried checking out the new owners of the Sweet Breeze place, but I couldn't get in. Have any bright ideas on how to enter?"

"Wait until the owners get back from work and ring the bell."

The waitress brought over his steak and eggs, and he pushed them around his plate while Kristy took quick bites of her omelet and finished her food.

"Sorry, I have a short lunch break." Kristy looked at him. "Hey, Winston, don't get so down. We'll work on this together if you still have misgivings. Cheer up. Hear that song?" She gave a jerk of her head toward the jukebox. He listened to the strains until he could identify "Chances Are."

"That could be our song. Let me leave some good luck with you." She grasped his hand with both of hers, the warmth of her fingers transferring over to his calloused knuckles. At the same time, he felt something cool laid against his dry and ridged palm.

"The spare key to my place," she said. "Do me a favor. Go and check on my cat, Blueberry, for me. I wouldn't dare trust him with anybody else."

She scribbled her address down on a napkin with the pink tip of her lipstick. After she left, he traced his finger across the digits tattooed in rose against the flimsy paper. His day was starting to look up.

CHAPTER 32

WINSTON DISTINGUISHED KRISTY'S home only by its number. She lived on the first floor in one of those apartments euphemistically labeled as condominiums. Its sole window gave a glassy stare at Winston as he marched up the steps with a plastic grocery bag swinging on his arm. He'd stopped by the convenience store for a quick treat for the cat, a tiny bag of dry kitten nibble that had cost him a fortune.

He opened the door to find a very tidy home inside. From the foyer, he could spy the majority of the layout. Everything seemed ready for a realtor's visit. Quiet nature prints, tasteful and conservative, lined the muted ivory walls. The couch held decorative square pillows, their gold tassels lying straight and combed down.

Winston took one step forward and almost tripped on the fluff ball of a cat lying in his path; it slinked toward the sunlight streaming in through the doorway, plopped down in a heap next to the frame, and purred.

"Blueberry?" Winston knelt down to pet the velveteen gray fur. The cat looked up for a moment, then started licking his paws and drew up into a fuzzy bowling ball shape. "I see where your name comes from. Well, I've got a treat for you." The cat stretched himself out and laid claim to the sunny spot, forcing Winston to leave the front door slightly ajar.

Winston moved into the kitchen, which smelled like lemons. Gleaming white mugs perched on a rack on the tiled countertop and looked ready for use. The ivory refrigerator didn't have a speck of dust on it—or the grimy fingerprints that marked his fridge at home. Stuck to the white expanse was a turquoise magnet clip that held two fat envelopes. Curious, he looked closer at them and saw that they both bore the same last name, "Blake," on their return addresses. She still kept in touch with her two younger brothers then. The postmarks (from New York and Oregon) indicated that she'd received the letters this month. Kristy seemed like the kind of woman who would still use snail mail and handwritten notes to stay connected.

A disgruntled meow from the other room reminded Winston of his intended task. He spotted two shiny steel bowls on the floor, engraved with "Blueberry." One held water. The other housed air. Winston opened the small bag of fancy cat food and filled the empty bowl to the brim. The clatter of pellets made Blueberry stroll to the kitchen and examine the gift offering. He nibbled a tiny piece, like a food critic. Then he took one massive paw and swiped the bowl, knocking kibble all over the tiled floor. Bits of dry cat food rolled under cabinet doors and the spotless fridge. Winston scrambled around and started using his hands to retrieve the runaway morsels. It took him a while to realize that a broom and dustpan would beat out cramped fingers.

While sweeping, he felt a sudden blast of cold air against his skin. He turned toward the front door. Why was it open wider than he remembered? Then he noticed the patch of sunlight where Blueberry had been lying—now empty. He rushed outside, calling the cat's name.

He scurried up and down the street, peering under the neighbors' hedges for a sign of gray fluff. He was surprised nobody called the cops on him. This was what he deserved for trying to cat-sit for Kristy. He had no experience with pets beyond the carnival fish he'd won in the first grade and subsequently flushed down the toilet when it died. His father had been deathly allergic to cats, any hint of fur causing the man to sneeze out hurricanes of snot and his eyes to water like a geyser. Besides which, his parents had also banned animals from the household because of their insistence on schoolwork being the number one priority of the family. No distractions allowed. That hadn't helped Winston too much on the academic front, though.

He stopped poking his head into bushes, sat down on Kristy's front steps and moaned. How could he face her without finding her beloved cat? He thought back to Blueberry's soft fur. Surely that breed of cat wasn't too hard to replicate. He could find a twin and maybe Kristy would never notice. There was only one place nearby to find a cat mill—in the pet store at the shopping center, Sunnyside Mall.

CHAPTER 33

SUNNYSIDE MALL, A tiny competitor in the world of chain malls, lay in south San Jose. It consisted of several drab brown buildings, and Winston wasn't sure if the color was due to the original paint or years of accumulated grime. The whole area held just two levels and was very walkable; at least Winston didn't get lost, as he often did wandering the Great Mall in Milpitas.

The center court held several containers of potted plants and a bubbling fountain with mounds of pennies collected at its bottom. Numerous security guards surrounded the central area. Winston wondered why until he saw a bevy of gorgeous women, all adorned in ethnic attire lined up behind heavy, velvet ropes. He spotted war paint on some, neck rings on others, and beaver hats adorning the rest of the beauties.

Telltale flashes of light bounced off reflecting screens, and he realized that they were waiting to be photographed. The huge banner above their heads read: "Modeling Contest: Exploring Cultures of the World, $1000 cash prize offered." As Winston scanned through the burst of clothing styles, his heart stopped. He spotted Carmen next in line. Here was his chance to get a lead in the murder case. She often visited Sweet Breeze and might have heard something important about the day Joe had died.

He waited while she twisted and twirled in her sari, long scarves trailing her arms like writhing snakes. After she stepped away from the camera's bright lights, he intercepted her.

"Hey, Carmen. Long time no see." He guided her away from the crowd, with a gentle hand on her elbow. She, possibly dazed by the bright lights of the flash photography, didn't resist, and Winston was glad to escape the watching eyes of the security without interference.

He led her to a hard wooden bench several yards from the center court, but she froze before the seat. "What are you doing here, Winston?"

"Taking a stroll at the local mall. How about you sit down and rest your pretty feet? I saw your lovely poses back there."

"I did do a good job, didn't I? The photographer told me I had the exotic vibe down."

"Beautiful costume."

"I know." Carmen giggled and covered her mouth with the tips of her fingers, a coy gesture. The little flurry of motion jiggled her bracelet. It reminded him of the one that had graced Anastasia's arm at Sweet Breeze.

"Where did you get that?" he asked.

She gave him a Mona Lisa smile. "Oh, wouldn't you like to know? Let's say it's from an admirer." She tossed her vibrant red hair.

"Not Rob Tuner, right?"

She pursed her lips at the name. "I wouldn't associate with a criminal."

He'd better get on her good side if he wanted any real information. "Do you think you'll win the contest, Carmen?"

"I will unless the judges are blind. I need the thousand dollars to kickstart my career."

"Modeling must be tough."

"It sure is," Carmen said.

"I don't know how you balance it all," Winston said. "Looking good and taking care of your family. Always visiting your nana at Sweet Breeze…"

Carmen shuddered, a little twist of her head and shoulders. "Poor Joe."

"You're a smart lady," Winston said. Carmen preened a little at the compliment. "Did you hear anything about what happened that day?"

"I don't want to talk about it." Carmen wrinkled her nose. "I think it's time for me to go."

Winston needed her to stay. How could he make her talk? She was the outsider at Sweet Breeze. So what if she was a wannabe model? Maybe she'd heard something helpful. If only he could offer her some bait, but what would spark her interest? "Wait a minute. Are you still pursuing acting?"

"I'm still looking for leads…"

Here was his way in. "You know, I have a friend in the industry."

"Really?"

It was a bit of the stretch to say that Alex handled movies, but it might work. "Well, he has a recording studio. It's for voice actors in video games."

She scanned Winston's face and then gave a brief nod. "That could work. When will he be free?"

"I can set up a session for three tomorrow afternoon." His friend should be awake by then. Winston crossed his fingers. He hoped Alex would be able to act on such quick notice.

"I'm open then. What's the address?"

He recited it by memory. Alex and Winston had been tight until the financial fall, and he still knew the man's contact info by heart.

"See you then, Winston." Carmen blew him a kiss and ambled off.

Winston dialed Alex's number and asked for the favor. It was a quick chat. He didn't have to worry because Alex was excited to have an actual model crossing his threshold after all these years. Besides, he did owe Winston a lot. He was the one who'd recommended the dot-coms that had killed Winston's financial portfolio. Winston had sunk so much money into the "guaranteed investments" that he'd never be able to retire, as far as he could see.

As he mulled over his lost brilliant financial future, his phone rang. Several shoppers turned around to glare at him. Winston's hearing had deteriorated over the years and now he had to set the cell's volume at the loudest level.

"Oh, hi Kri—"

"What did you do, Winston? The kitchen's a mess, and I can't find Blueberry anywhere."

"Oh, you're home." Crap. She had found out, and he hadn't even started looking for a replacement feline yet.

"What happened?" Kristy asked.

"I was getting him food—"

"Why isn't he here?"

"He was in the way of the door. I couldn't close it."

"You're not making any sense," Kristy said. "Just tell me the simple facts."

"Well, um, he ran out the door when I wasn't looking."

Kristy groaned. "No! He's a housecat. He's always stayed inside. How will he survive?"

"I'm not sure." Winston didn't know the first thing about cats—or women, it seemed. Maybe he could tell a joke and move on. "Don't cats have nine lives, anyway?"

"Not funny, Winston. Blueberry suffers from high blood pressure."

He'd never heard of that before. "Are you serious?"

She huffed at him and hung up the phone. Guess cats did get chronic illnesses. He put his head in his hands. He'd screwed up with Kristy again, and he wasn't sure how to fix the situation. He sighed. Maybe something miraculous would happen, just like his run-in with Carmen today. He would have to tuck away his relationship issues in the back of his mind and compartmentalize his life. He needed to stay focused when Carmen met up with his friend Alex tomorrow.

CHAPTER 34

WINSTON'S FRIEND ALEX rented a townhouse close to the San Jose State campus. In the glare of the afternoon sun, the building's pistachio green walls seemed to give off an almost alien fluorescence. The place must have seen better days, a time when the glaring color had been a symbol of fashion. Still, the tri-level townhouse operated under rent control, a fact Alex happily embraced when his own investments (the same ones he'd suggested to Winston) went under.

Alex used to lead Winston under his senior QA position (Winston thought the "quality assurance" abbreviation should've been replaced by the simpler "tester" label). When Alex's savings failed, he got work recording voice actors. Unlike Winston, he'd landed back on his feet through networking. Alex sure knew how to schmooze his way in the gaming industry.

In fact, Winston found Alex charming Carmen with compliments about her voice when he entered. "You've got a beautiful tone that everyone needs to hear recorded." Alex shuffled around setting up and testing his equipment. He'd dressed himself special for the occasion, wearing a soft V-neck sweater, no doubt hiding a free gaming convention T-shirt underneath.

"Let's set you up, sweetheart." He adjusted her chair, so that it swiveled closer to the microphone.

"How long have you been doing this, Alex?" Carmen asked.

"Over ten years." Winston heard a slight crack in his voice, the only indication his mind had briefly touched upon his financial shame. When he resumed talking, Alex spoke a bit louder. "Don't worry, doll, I'm a professional."

Carmen crossed her arms, boosting up her well-endowed chest over her top's neckline. "What's the last project you worked on?"

Alex named a couple of major recent hits he'd been involved in. "Today, we're recording for a game called *Women Warriors*. It's kind of like *Mortal Kombat*, but filled with females."

Carmen tossed her head, a mass of fire-hot curls dancing in the sunlight. "I know all about it. I'm a gamer myself."

"A hottie like you?" Alex stopped fiddling with the microphone. "Sorry, it just slipped out. I can't believe you'd spend time glued to the screen when you could be lighting up a night club."

"I can keep up with both lifestyles. Sometimes I think I could even star in an *eroge*."

Alex let out a long wolf whistle. "I bet you could. You even look part Asian." Winston himself shied away from those very erotic Japanese anime games. "So are you single?" Alex asked. Trust him to do pleasure before business.

She looked Alex over. Even to Winston, a polished-up Alex wasn't half bad-looking, with his tousled hazel hair and amber eyes. "Here's my contact info, stud." Winston craned his neck and did a double take. He recognized the address: 2255 Julian Street. Could it be just a coincidence? He needed to get into the place again and search for more clues. Maybe he'd missed something crucial the first time around.

"Ready to test this baby out?" Alex asked Carmen.

"Sure thing. Testing one-two-three."

"You'll have to get closer." Alex placed a hand and urged Carmen forward in her seat. "Why don't you put that purse down and grab the mike with both hands?"

Seeing nowhere to put it on the tabletop, Carmen plopped the purse below her mesh computer chair.

"Here are the lines you need to read." He held several sheets in front of her face.

While Carmen read, Winston edged closer. His eyes remained locked onto the recording process like a good bystander, but his feet swept forward to grab the purse. Good thing he'd taken off his flip-flops, like a good Asian boy, when he'd entered the home. His bare toes pinched the bag and dragged it toward him. He sat down, cross-legged, and rifled through its contents, his motions covered up by Carmen's loud, enunciated speaking. He'd fished out the house key and kicked the purse back under the stool when Carmen stopped talking. She turned around in her chair and asked, "What are you doing on the ground, Winston?"

"I'm resting." Winston's hand—the one covering the key—swiveled in a tiny arc across the plush carpet. "This floor's so nice. I almost want to take a nap here."

"No can do, buddy," Alex said. "I don't want to record the sound of your snoring in the background. Why don't you grab a cup of coffee? In the kit—"

"Great idea! I'll make a Starbucks run and get some food, too."

Stomachs growling, they agreed and placed their orders with him. Winston took off to the hardware store first, then dropped by the coffee shop and fished out a couple of sandwiches from the refrigerated section. While standing in line, though, he noticed Kristy and Mark Gaffey in a corner table. She kept glancing down at her coffee, swirling it with a swizzle stick and looking back at the cop again.

Every time she looked up at Mark, Winston could feel knots tying up his stomach. He could only imagine what Mark was feeling as Kristy's luxurious lashes flicked upwards and uncovered her beautiful brown eyes.

The barista had to get his attention twice when it came time to place his coffee order. Good thing they made drinks fast because he couldn't wait to escape the shop and an overwhelming sense of betrayal.

Although he shook with anger, Winston still had enough concentration to make it back to Alex's place. He entered with three cups of coffee and a couple of gourmet sandwiches in his hands. He placed them in the dining area, a granite countertop surrounded by black leather barstools. He reached into his pants pocket, checking to make sure that two identical keys lay there.

Winston walked over to the recording equipment. "All done?" he asked.

Carmen sat facing him, arms clutched around her purse. "I'm ready to go."

"She's a natural, Winston. We breezed through the recordings."

"Thanks, Alex," Carmen said. She pecked Alex on the cheek, leaving a magenta stain on his clean-shaven face.

"It was my great pleasure. I'll let you know when the product's done. Maybe I'll host a party to celebrate."

"I'd like that." She nodded her head at Winston. "I'll eat my food on the road. Later, Winston."

Carmen swooped up her sandwich and coffee and moved to the exit where Winston intercepted her. He grabbed her wrist. "Wait, don't go. It's nicer to sit down and enjoy your meal."

"No, I should get home before Nana worries about me."

"He's right, Carmen," Alex said. "It's better to eat well, digest your food, and keep your car clean. Besides, isn't it unsafe to eat and drive? You're welcome to stay here as long as you want."

As Carmen looked back and forth between the two men, Winston said, "Oh, I see how it is. Three's a crowd." Then he launched himself at Alex but turned at the last moment, so that his shoulder only grazed Alex's chest. He didn't want to actually hurt his friend; he just needed to pretend fight. Even so, Alex got knocked around a little.

"Ugh," Alex said. "What's wrong with you, man?"

Winston pushed him down, but Alex attempted to scramble up and almost knocked over his own recording equipment. "Go with it," Winston mouthed.

"Be careful!" Carmen said. She ran over to them, dropping her purse, and attempted to break up the fight. Winston wasn't sure if she was more worried about her precious work being lost or their potential broken bones.

Winston and Alex moved out of her reach and rolled around several times on the floor.

"You need to stop, boys. It's silly to fight over me," Carmen said, even as a smile ghosted her lips.

Winston grabbed the purse during the acrobatics and whacked Alex with it, unlocking the button along the way. Its contents spilled all over the plush carpet, and Winston stopped fighting. "Oh, I'm so sorry, Carmen."

He scrambled on all fours to gather the things near him: loose tissues and old receipts. Out of the corner of his eye, he saw Alex and Carmen also trying to recover fleeing lipstick containers and stray breath mints. While they were busy, he slipped the original house key out of his pocket and into the miscellaneous items in his hands. He thrust it all back into Carmen's purse.

Winston clutched at his back. "I'm too old for this, Alex," he said. "Our five-year age gap makes a lot of physical difference."

"That's right, Grandpa." Alex pinned Winston's neck in a headlock and whispered in his ear. "I don't know what the hell you're doing, but I went along with it. In my book, this will make us even forever."

Once Winston could breathe again after Alex's tight grip, he apologized to Carmen. "Sorry, I overreacted."

"Don't worry," she said. "I see it as a taste of what my future adoring fans will be like when I win that modeling contest and get featured in *Women Warriors*." She left with a huge smile on her face.

As he made his way to his own car, Winston rubbed his fingers over the precious piece of metal in his pocket. A sudden vibration from his other pocket made him freeze, though. Had he been found out? He looked at his offending cell phone and recognized his sister's caller ID.

"Hey, Winston, where are you?" Marcy asked.

"What do you mean?" Why was his sister calling him now? At least, he was glad it wasn't Carmen figuring out he'd duplicated her key.

"I'm here at the airport," Marcy said. "Did you forget I was coming?"

He did, but he wasn't about to admit that to her. "I'm stuck in traffic," he said.

"I've already been waiting for twenty minutes."

"Be there in no time," Winston said and crossed his fingers.

CHAPTER 35

WINSTON'S SISTER MARCY spun around the mother-in-law suite surveying the room. She narrowed her eyes when she saw the electric blue inflatable chairs. Apparently, the fake leather throws hadn't thrown off their aura of cheapness. "Do you honestly expect me to sleep in here?"

Winston noticed that Marcy's hand-embroidered floral suitcase still had its handle up, as if she was ready to bolt. They'd been there fifteen minutes already, and she hadn't settled in yet. "It'll give you more privacy," he said. "It's got its own entrance and everything."

Marcy hooked her hands onto her hips. "Winston, there isn't a bed in here."

He scratched his head and pulled away a gray hair. He hid it out of sight. How come Marcy didn't have any white hairs? She was five years older than him. "Um, I think I've got a sleeping bag in the garage."

"I'm not sleeping on the floor." She started pulling her suitcase along and entered the main house.

Winston followed her mincing steps, her genuine leather heels clicking a military pace. He watched the back of her tailored black suit walk around like she owned the place, which of course, she did. Winston saw her open a door in the hallway a tiny crack. "Hey, that's my room."

He saw her nose wrinkle up as she slammed the door. "What do you keep in there? Skunks?" She went down the corridor some more. "Aren't there two more rooms in your home?"

One was filled with tons of electronics. Some were broken pieces of computers that he'd meant to refurbish. Other things were intact but useless, like his crates of Atari games that he kept for nostalgia's sake.

The second room was filled with boxes. He kept all his financial papers in there, tons of documents about his previous failed investments. Tax documents. Random receipts. Marcy chewed on her lip. "You would think that with all this space, you'd have one guest room ready."

"I don't have people over."

"I can see that." She wiped a layer of dust from one of the cardboard containers. "I can also tell that you forgot about my visit."

"C'mon, Marcy. You know this is unusual. You don't typically have time to chitchat in my house. I'm normally a tight coffee squeeze on one of your conference days."

"Well, this time I flew in one day early to see my little brother."

"I know. Thanks for thinking of me." He saw her press a finger against the side of her nose to stifle a sneeze, so he led her away from the dusty room. "What about the den?"

Winston plumped the pillows on the futon in the den. Good thing his sister had a petite four-foot-eleven frame. She would fit on the tiny mattress. "It's not the Westin, but at least it's a bed. It'll have to do until tomorrow when you get to check into your fancy hotel."

"I didn't say anything negative about the futon."

"Your thoughts were so loud I could you hear you thinking them."

"Don't be so defensive, Winston. You don't need my approval."

"Don't I?" Winston crossed his arms and glared at his sister. "Tell me the truth, Marcy. What's the real reason you came out? Maybe it's to check on your housing investment."

Marcy snapped the handle down on her luggage. "What are you talking about?"

"The property you bought, this house. I think you're just fishing to see how it turned out, and you're not impressed."

"You're a bachelor. What else could I have expected?" She stowed her suitcase under the coffee table; the luggage's pretty petal embroidery looked distorted through the murky, scratched glass surface.

"I'm sorry I'm not perfect like you with your solid career, a sprawling mansion, and a doting spouse."

"Shut up." Marcy's voice rose an octave. *"Ding lay go fai."*

Hit your lungs? He scratched his head. His Cantonese needed some brushing up. Marcy excelled at the language, though he normally knew curses and put-downs pretty well, having heard them directed at him all his life via his mother. Ah, that's right. Lungs played a role in the literal definition, but "go to hell" was the better English equivalent.

"You didn't have to bail me out like a little kid, Marcy."

His sister clenched her hands into fists and counted to ten (in Cantonese) under her breath. Her snipped words came out between heaving breaths. "I wanted to partner with you and help you, not bail you out."

"It was a rescue mission, Marcy. You know I couldn't put in squat, not after my money troubles..." Winston squished the throw pillow, its stuffing squirting out through the broken seam.

"Of course, you wouldn't know anything about that. Money takes care of all your problems."

"You don't know the half—" A doorbell stopped her talking, and the anger seemed to drain out of her with the prospect of a stranger. She took off her heels and settled down on the couch. "Get the door," she said. Her voice sounded muffled with the frayed throw pillow over her head.

Winston turned to the front door. Didn't those salespeople see his "No Soliciting" sign? He opened it to find Kristy on his doorstep. "Hey," she said. "I'm sorry I got mad at you about the cat."

"You don't blame me for Blueberry disappearing?"

"Well, he came back to me this morning. Officer Gaffey found him wandering the streets, looked at the tags, and located me. I bought him a drink at Starbucks in thanks." That explained coffee with a cop from this afternoon. Maybe it was nothing more than a gesture of gratitude.

"I took Blueberry to the vet to get him checked out." Kristy almost nibbled on one of her perfect moon-shaped nails but stopped herself in time. "She told me that he should get out more often. It seems like exercise really helps to lower his blood pressure. So I actually owe you for letting my cat see the neighborhood."

"You're welcome, I think."

"Maybe we can take Blueberry outside together sometime. I would feel so silly walking a cat alone."

Thank goodness she was still planning a future together with him. "I'd love to. You know, you didn't have to come over to apologize. You could have just called me."

"I got off work early to make it up to you." She thrust a bag of groceries into his face. "I wanted to make dinner for you."

He juggled the laden paper bag back and forth between his hands. "By the way, my sister's visiting for the evening."

Kristy shrugged. "Oh good, I would like to meet your family. The more, the merrier."

CHAPTER 36

WINSTON AND KRISTY walked over to the couch, where Marcy's head remained buried under the pillow. Winston prodded his sister in the stomach.

"Stop it." She groaned, a prolonged soft whistle. "I'm trying to rest here."

"Sis, we've got company."

Marcy sat straight up and smoothed back her tousled hair. "Oh, hello." She extended her hand to Kristy. "I'm Marcy, Winston's sister."

Kristy introduced herself. Then she glanced sideways at Winston. "Your brother and I are sort of seeing each other."

Did that mean they were serious? Winston halted his automatic fist pump, as he noticed his sister swivel her head toward him. She raised an eyebrow, and he gave her a quick nod. Yeah, I got a girl.

Kristy rearranged the pillow behind Marcy's head. "Do you have a headache? Would you like a cool compress?"

"No, no." She waved the ministrations away. "I'll be fine."

"Well, why don't you sit back and let me cook dinner? Winston, you can help me prep the ingredients."

He helped "cook" the salad, one of the few items he couldn't mess up. There was something intimate about being in the kitchenette together. The way the tiny space filled up with tantalizing smells and the fiery heat closing them in.

They dug in minutes after the spread was laid out on the table: honey-glazed pork chops, buttered corn on the cob, a Caesar salad, and fresh baked bread. The dishes Kristy made tasted better than any he'd ever eaten at a fancy restaurant. He chowed down while the girls talked shop. Kristy spoke about her nursing work with seniors, while Marcy droned on about her research and her numerous speaking engagements.

He looked at his empty plate and realized that one thing was missing. He found a carton of green tea ice cream in the back of the freezer and pried it open. Iced over, but still fine. He scooped some out for everybody. After dessert, he burped and patted his stomach. Compliments to the chef.

Unfortunately, the chef's eyes started blinking with sleep, so Winston led Kristy to the front door. He felt his sister behind him and decided to give Kristy a chaste peck on the cheek instead of the longer kiss he'd intended. He whispered in Kristy's ear. "You don't know how much you saved me back there from my sister's griping." Louder, he said, "Drive carefully."

After the door closed, Marcy said, "Buddha belly, let's clear the table and wash up—by hand." She pointed to the bamboo drying rack on the kitchen countertop. "You're so Asian. I know you use that dishwasher on the side for storage only."

They divided the work, with Winston scrubbing and Marcy rinsing. She'd taken off her suit jacket and was left standing in her silk camisole. He noted a mark, the size of a dime, on her upper right arm. Winston recoiled. "What's that?"

He gripped his sister's arm and stared. "Wait a minute." He remembered another figure-eight mark—on a dead body. It was the exact shape and color as Joe's had been. "How did you get that?"

She tried to pull away, but he held on. "Please, Marcy, tell me."

She sighed. "It's there for some medicine I'm taking."

"Medicine?" His sister had an illness? Now, he recalled that Ruisa, Marcy's botanist friend, had talked about some pills. He snapped his fingers. "Valerian, right?"

"What?" She laughed. "I see Ruisa must have passed the message on to you. She can't understand why I'm taking this new-age medicine, but valerian alone doesn't work for me. The stress doesn't disappear like it does with this enhancer."

"You're stressed out?" Winston let go of her arm.

"You might think I have the perfect life, but you don't know the half of it."

Winston tsked at her. "All your work and traveling."

She flung the water from her hands at him. "You're so blind. It's about having kids. Gary's always wanted them and we just couldn't…"

"I never knew, Marcy," Winston said. "I thought you were so busy with work that you two opted not to have kids."

"I let you think that. It was easier on me, not to worry you. The truth is, I go to all these conferences to get away from the problems at home."

Winston turned on the faucet, rinsing away the bubbles on his hands and in the sink. "I don't get it. Can't you use some fancy biotechnology to make kids instead of taking stress relievers?"

She laughed in a shattered voice. "Winston, I'm forty-five. I'm not going to have kids now. Besides, Gary wanted everything natural. And no, we never talked about adoption."

Winston put his arm around her shoulder. "Since the kiddies stage has passed, can't you two move on?"

"It's harder than it looks. The worst part is seeing friends' kids grow up and trying to act happy in front of them." She rubbed at the mark on her arm. "This new drug helps me. It's pretty natural, and it acts like a booster for any medicine, making the ingredients three times as potent, so I combine it with the valerian. I pay a ton more to just get the enhancer in the set."

"I'm not following you. Is there a combo involved?"

"The company, Sana Technologies—"

"Haven't I seen that name somewhere?"

"They're on billboards all across the city." He remembered the name gracing a sign next to the old Sweet Breeze building. "Anyway, they've created a combo dementia treatment. There's the booster portion and the medicine part, and it's packaged together for dementia patients." She unzipped her suitcase and pulled out a slender silver tube labeled, "Marcy Wong."

Winston grabbed the vial out of her hands and examined it. This could be a vital clue in his case. But he couldn't even figure out how to open the thing.

"Wow," Marcy said. "I never knew you were so concerned about my welfare."

Winston gave his sister back her medication. "Sorry, I snatched it from you." Maybe it was better to play along with her assumption, though. She would provide more info if she thought he was the sympathetic little brother.

"I'm wondering," Winston said. "How did you get that mark on your arm?"

"It's harmless, Winston. It's from the company, Sana Technologies. Do you see the 'S' symbol?" Oh, it was supposed to be a letter, not a figure eight. "It's a temporary tattoo, so I can find the right injection site."

"I don't know anything about medicine, Marcy."

"You put it where you want to inject the booster, so that it'll absorb properly."

Winston touched his sister's tattoo. A birthmark on a dead man resembling the tattoo used by a company offering a new dementia drug. What were the chances it was a coincidence? Winston was no longer a betting man, but he'd have staked some cash on those odds.

"Stop thinking about it," Marcy said. She swatted his hand away. "I'm totally fine, and it'll come off in about five days." She ruffled his hair, like he was kid again. "By the way, I liked your new girlfriend."

"Kristy, yeah, she's great."

"What a nice woman. I can't believe she cooked dinner for us and everything. She's pretty, too, with her raven hair and porcelain skin. Don't mess this one up."

"I won't. I promise," Winston said. His sister had just reminded him. Kristy would know the ins and outs of Eve's medications. Maybe she could tie the case to Carmen, who was now the happy possessor of the old Sweet Breeze home. "Actually, I need to make a phone call to Kristy now. I'll thank her for dinner and stuff."

For privacy, Winston retreated to his room to place the call.

"Hello?" Kristy's voice was groggy. He'd probably pulled her out of bed. His mind dwelled on an image of her soft sheets a beat too long. "Winston, I have caller ID. I know it's you."

He refocused on the conversation. "Kristy, thanks for dinner… And I have a question for you. Did Eve have any new drugs for her dementia? Something from Sana Technologies?"

"The name doesn't ring a bell." It wouldn't be so easy to trace the connection to Carmen then. "Why?"

"I'll tell you later when I get more info. Go back to sleep, Kristy."

He hung up and searched for his sister. She was getting ready for bed. "Your conference starts in the afternoon, right?" She nodded. "How about a field trip bright and early tomorrow?"

CHAPTER 37

SANA TECHNOLOGIES TOOK up all six floors of the mirrored building. Winston and Marcy stood looking at its imposing structure from the parking lot.

"I don't know why you wanted a tour, anyway. It's all above board," Marcy said. She shook her head. "I know what medications are appropriate. I'm a professional, remember?"

"Humor me," Winston said. He needed to go inside to get the scoop on this new drug. It might prove to be the key to his case.

Sana Technologies' shiny exterior reflected back the sun's harsh rays, so that Winston stumbled as he walked into the slick marble interior. The ice blonde receptionist (her hair as well as her temperament) eyed Winston with distrust. "This is a private company," she said.

"My sister's taking one of your drugs—"

The receptionist scowled at Winston. "We don't work with patients directly here. Call the 1-800 number on the medicine with your complaints."

Marcy nudged Winston to the side, whispering in his ear first, "Let me handle it." She straightened her posture and addressed the receptionist. "I'm Marcy Wong. I recently published an article about the cross-disciplinary effects of DM-160 with herbal remedies and its ramifications on public consumption."

The receptionist's mouth hung open. "What did you say? Are you a doctor?"

"Tell Lewis Crate that Dr. Wong is here," Marcy said. "He'll know who I am."

"Right away." The receptionist dialed Crate's extension and announced them. After she hung up, the receptionist said, "Dr. Crate is waiting for you in his office. He said that you'll know the way from your last visit."

They reached Crate's office using a ten-second elevator speed ride. The placard outside his office read, "Lewis Crate, Ph.D. Director of Scientific Research." On the top floor, Crate's view consisted of the roofs of nearby buildings. When Winston met Crate, he imagined that towering over others was his typical view; the man had to be at least six foot seven. The sandy-haired man grinned at Marcy and shook hands with Winston using a strong grip. Crate then turned to Winston's sister. "Marcy Wong, to what do I owe this pleasure?"

"My brother Winston is interested in learning more about your medication, DM-160."

"How does it work, Dr. Crate?" Winston asked. The doctor, excited at a captive audience, droned on and on about the medication. In the end, Winston came away with the same facts that Marcy had already given him. DM-160 was given as a shot; part of it was a booster and part of it was the actual medication. How could the man keep all those chemical compounds straight in his mind? Could Crate see that Winston didn't understand a word he was saying? Winston licked his lips; he did that whenever he was nervous.

"Thirsty?" Crate poured out two glasses of chilled Evian water for his guests.

"Why the specific interest in DM-160, though? Do you know someone who has Alzheimer's? Or…you seemed dazed back there." Crate held the frosted bottle aloft, his bicep bulging through the thin shirt, an advertisement of his youth. "Have you noticed some symptoms yourself, Winston?"

"My mind is working fine." Winston took a gulp from his water glass and imagined spitting it out at Crate. "I'm here in regards to a patient of yours."

Marcy nudged Winston. "You don't have to be so formal." She looked at Crate and grinned. "Actually, since I'm a patient of yours, my little brother is worried—"

Winston spoke over his sister. "It's for an investigation I'm working on."

Marcy gave Winston her look of death. It was the one that had reduced her peers to tears during the school years, when she'd carried home all those math and science awards. Like the optic blast from Cyclops.

Crate put the water down and examined Winston. "Are you a police officer?" His hands trembled a little. "Or with the IRS?"

"A private detective."

"Ah." Crate gave an indulgent smile and crossed his legs. "Do go on."

"I wanted to know if a woman named Eve Solstice received DM-160 from your company."

"Tsk, tsk, Detective." Crate shook his finger at Winston. "I can't reveal confidential client information."

Marcy chimed in. "Yes, I don't think he should either. Winston, it's not like you even have a real detective bad—"

Winston stepped on Marcy's toe with his sneaker (he'd exchanged his usual flip-flops for formal shoe wear on this occasion). He caught her on that vulnerable exposed skin area right above her pumps, and she gave a little yelp. Winston started talking again before she could recover. "I'm in the process of starting my detective career, as my dear sister knows."

Crate looked back and forth between Marcy and Winston, but wisely kept his mouth shut.

"Excuse us, Lewis. It's time for my brother and I to leave." Marcy said this while rubbing her foot. She started practically dragging Winston away, but he wasn't going to leave when he was so close to getting more information. He aimed a pinch at the "S" mark on her arm (thank goodness for short-sleeved dress suits). She was still sore at the injection site and let him go.

Lewis checked his watch. "I do need to get back to work. See you at a future conference, Marcy." He gave Winston a hard stare. "Have a good day, Detective."

Winston nodded at him and left with Marcy. Once outside, she faced him with her hands on her hips. "You're in big trouble."

"When am I not with you?"

"Why is everything a joke to you? I embarrassed myself back there." Her face started getting red, but she checked her watch and began taking deep breaths. "I need to speak at the convention in less than an hour."

Thank goodness Marcy needed full concentration and couldn't afford to be flustered at the podium. Maybe he could even barter with her. "Too bad you didn't rent a car. How about you forgive me, and I give you the ride you need?"

"Maybe I'll hail a cab."

Winston looked around the parking lot and on the main street. Not a circling taxi in sight. "This isn't NYC, sis."

"Why didn't you tell me this tour was for your case?" Marcy asked. She had moved from pure rage to a hint of sadness. "I thought you were worried about me."

"I am. It's still sad about you and Gary." Winston paused. He wasn't sure that he sounded sincere enough to her. After all, he'd just been fishing for information back at Sana Technologies and had pinched her.

Marcy raised her eyebrows at him. It didn't look like she believed a word he was saying. He tried to pat her shoulder in sympathy, but it looked a little like he was just pulling lint off her suit. He needed to make her understand. They were siblings through it all, and they were stuck with each other for life (the only ones of their family left).

"You know I need this case," Winston said. "Mom and Dad were right. The video game stuff didn't work out for me. I need to make sure this detective thing succeeds."

"Men," Marcy said, swatting his hand away from her shoulder, where he was continuing his ineffectual patting.

Winston was betting on habit, her usual protocol of rescuing her dorky little brother. He needed her help, and that was like a siren call for her personality. Marcy bit her lip, but she made her way to the car and opened the door.

She got inside but before buckling, she looked over at him. "What else are you gonna give me?"

Whenever he'd screwed up in the past, he'd had to make it up to her with treats, bribes, something. "I promise to redo the house," Winston said. "You can stay over whenever you want—in a proper room."

"I get to choose the color scheme and the furnishings."

"Deal." They used their secret handshake, a combination of some girly patty cake move and a manly fist bump. He breathed a sigh of relief—they were okay…for now.

He dropped her off at the herbology convention without further incident and dialed Kristy in the hotel parking lot.

"Can you help me out?" Winston asked. "Who's Eve's primary physician, and where's his office?"

"I can't quite remember. I think the name starts with a 'D,' though."

Winston thumped his hand against the steering wheel. How else could he proceed? He decided to ask Kristy for the previous Sweet Breeze residents' new locations. Time to make the rounds again and grill the eyewitnesses. Ladies first, he decided.

CHAPTER 38

ANASTASIA LIVED AT the Silicon Valley Skilled Nursing Facility. It looked like a hospital with its imposing concrete structure. Sliding glass doors opened onto a world of white walls. The fierce air conditioning made Winston shiver, and he wondered if they used the cold air to decrease the odor of stale urine. The place would require nose plugs if the smell was left to ripen in warm stuffiness.

He stepped up to the nurse at the front station. "I'm looking for the Russian princess who stays here." He had no doubt Anastasia had already impressed the workers with her royal lineage, but the woman gave her bushy head a shake. Her black curls flew out like Medusa's snakes, even hissing in the air. "No such person. I need her name, please."

"Anastasia. She recently transferred here from Sweet Breeze."

The nurse pulled out a roster sheet. "Let me look at the admittance dates. Found it. Now, sign here." She stuck a clipboard in his face, and he filled out the visitor info sheet.

"Where do I go?"

"Down that corridor." She jerked her thumb to the right. "101C."

He wandered around the hallway and then circled back before finding Room 101. He wasn't sure what the "C" part meant until he entered the cramped space. Apparently, Anastasia's room was split into three sections, one for each of its inhabitants. The resident closest to the door, slot "A," was not in her space. The second roommate, stuck in the middle "B" position, slept deeply. A high-pitched snoring hung in the air like a siren.

He found Anastasia, resident C, tucked near the back wall. She occupied a rusted hospital bed, which looked like it would splinter into pieces. A crooked over-the-bed table held a glass of water, which threatened to spill from its precarious position. He tried to steady the drink.

"Forget about it, Winston. It'll be fine," Anastasia said. "Thanks for visiting."

"How are you doing, Anastasia?" Winston eyed the room. Its smallness felt claustrophobic compared to Sweet Breeze. He couldn't believe her princess personality was reduced to this lowly place. And perhaps all for nothing, if he'd pointed the finger at the wrong man.

"Want to hear something funny?" Anastasia said. "You know the residents' nickname for this place?" He shook his head. "House for Survivors, they call it," she said. "First, I thought it was because all of us are so old. Then I realized we weren't surviving life, but this place." Now he felt even worse about the whole thing.

"I'm sorry you couldn't stay at Sweet Breeze—it was so spacious there," Winston said. "It had a real sense of community. When I asked the nurse up front to lead me to the Russian princess, she had no idea whom I was talking about."

"The nurses often forget our names, but that's not why she didn't know." Anastasia flipped one hand in the air, like she was swatting at a fly. "I don't use that line about my fake heritage anymore."

"Really?" Winston eyed the glittering entourage of jewels lined up on her fingers.

She followed his gaze. "That doesn't mean I don't still dress with flair. I just don't need to lie about my birth origin. Being an orphan is A-okay with folks in these parts." She snorted. "Half the residents don't even remember my background anyway."

Anastasia smoothed the buttery chiffon shawl wrapped around her shoulders. "So is this purely a social call, Winston? You should have told me earlier… I would've put on more makeup." She patted her face, which already held a heavy layer of pale powder.

"I'm afraid not, Anastasia. I'm still investigating Joe's death."

She stopped preening before him. "What do you mean? Isn't Rob behind bars awaiting a trial?" She licked her lips, as though tasting something delicious. "Wait a minute. Did he escape?"

"No, it's nothing like that. I think Joe's death might have been more complicated than I first thought." Winston told her about how the police didn't find any poison in the vial from Rob's mini fridge. "Can you go over the day of Joe's death once more, Anastasia? Tell me about who was gathered there to celebrate your birthday."

She tapped her hand against the slanted table. Her costume rings clinked against its plastic surface. "Nobody unusual. Rob, Kristy, the other residents."

She stopped drumming her fingers. "Oh, Carmen was there, too. She always wants to be center of attention, but you can't upstage the birthday girl."

Carmen was at Sweet Breeze the day Joe had died, which meant she'd had the opportunity to take his life. "I need to go, Anastasia," Winston said.

As he exited the nursing facility, Winston saw a giant US flag waving from across the street. Two letters popped into sight: VA. He double-checked the address. Perfect. Looked like it was time to visit Pete Russell.

CHAPTER 39

THE VA HOUSING unit displayed an efficient look due to its chrome structure. It ran like a modern-day hospital, with its staff traipsing up and down the hallways. Winston couldn't even begin to count all the doctors, nurses, psychologists, physical and occupational therapists, their clipboards in hand, off to visit various rooms.

Pete Russell's room also emitted a hospital vibe, but it was a separate unit, unlike Anastasia's. Two recliners surrounded the hospital bed, as though every resident received multiple visitors a day. Pete gestured to one of the mustard yellow seats. "Come on in, Winston. Make yourself at home."

The room's open window let in a refreshing breeze. A pitcher of ice-cold water, not even sweating in the heat, along with an array of snacks lay beside Pete on his bedside table.

"You've got a nice place here," Winston said.

"Yeah." Pete grunted. "It only took five years to get off the wait list."

"I'd sign up in a heartbeat, too, if I qualified."

Pete pulled out his deck of cards from under the crisp, white bedsheet. "Are you here for a quick game because you owe me one?"

Winston moved his recliner closer. "Sure, deal me in, but you'll have to answer my questions at the same time."

"No problem. I can play War in my sleep." Pete split the deck into two piles.

Winston took his half. "I'm changing my mind about Rob being the one involved in Joe's murder."

Pete whistled a tuneless snippet. "You don't say."

"Carmen's the main suspect now." Winston placed a two of hearts on the bed, while Pete won with an eight of clubs.

"The ditzy model? Are you sure she could pull off something like that?"

"I know her new address. She lives at the Sweet Breeze house," Winston said. "Housing is a great motive for murder."

"Well, she did act strange the day Joe died."

"You saw something odd?"

"She didn't look at Joe's body."

"What was she doing instead?"

"She was hunched over, looking at the floor." Pete swept off all the cards on the bed, the clear winner, and stacked them. "I figured she just didn't want to see a dead body. Young people don't like to stare mortality in the face."

"Hmm, that is strange behavior." What had Carmen really been looking for in Joe's room? "One more thing, Pete. Did you notice if her clothes were wet?" He figured if Rob had sliced open the dialysis bags, Carmen might have gotten some of the remaining liquid on her.

"No, I didn't notice that." He chuckled. "Not much chance, though, with what she was wearing—a spaghetti strap tank top and a mini skirt."

Pete packed all the cards back in the box. "You should go see Jazzman, though. He might have some photos from that day, and you can see for yourself. The man's a real picture hog when he performs on special occasions." Winston remembered the photos that had hung around Jazzman's old room. "Besides, it was Anastasia's birthday that day. She made a big fuss over it, even telling Kristy to bake a cake for her, so she probably made him take a picture of the party."

Concrete photographic evidence from Jazzman? "Thank you so much, Pete." After the wall with Sana Technologies, things were starting to look up for Winston.

CHAPTER 40

GENTLE PASTURES RESIDENCE, a mere two streets from the old Sweet Breeze home, took its green reference to extremes. Olive green exterior paint, about the color of dried mucus, coated the little house. Inside, the walls were a clean mint green, constantly reminding Winston to check himself for bad breath and yearn for chewing gum. Even the abundant supply of carpet covering the floor displayed a dark forest green hue. Winston felt like he'd entered a jungle, except for the humans walking around the environment.

Once he found Jazzman's room, he relaxed. The walls were a normal white. Of course, Jazzman had already hung up such an array of photos they would have covered over any indecent green paint job.

"Winston, nice of you to visit me."

"Any time, Jazzman." Winston noted the feather bed and cozy armchairs. "You've found yourself in another beautiful home."

"It's nice, except for the split pea soup colors. Besides, they don't have a piano here, so it can't compare with Sweet Breeze."

"Speaking of which, Pete suggested I come by here to see you."

"Really? How's he doing?"

"Pete's in veterans' housing now, and I think he's feeling more understood there."

"Good for him. I only got in here because my family and some ex-fans put up some money for me. It costs a pretty penny for assisted living."

Winston walked around and touched the frames on the wall, each already dusted and polished. "Pete tells me you had your picture taken at Sweet Breeze every time you played the piano for an event."

"I like to commemorate the special occasions," he said.

"Do you think you have one from the day Joe died?"

"I do. In fact, I was looking through them the other day." Jazzman lifted his bedspread, revealing that his mattress was raised on concrete blocks. "I stick my stuff underneath here."

"Let me give you a hand," Winston said. The space underneath was filled with cardboard boxes. Two-thirds of them contained vinyl records, each labeled in a familiar neat script. "Did Kristy help you with packing?"

"She sure did. She keeps me organized." Jazzman peered at the remainder of boxes, all containing photos. He examined their written dates and pulled the lid off one. "I know there's fancy digital stuff nowadays, but I like pictures I can hold onto. There aren't too many of that day, I'm afraid." He handed three pictures over.

Winston flipped through them. One picture of Jazzman standing at the piano, dressed up with a golden brocade vest over a white button-down shirt with his top hat in hand. Another featured Anastasia blowing out the candles on a lopsided cake, a vanilla confectionary topped with fresh strawberries. The last one was taken of the party participants all together. Everyone smiled at the camera, except for Eve, who was gripping her granddaughter's hand tightly, with Carmen half-turned toward her and partially gesturing at the lens.

"The funny thing was my nurse recognized Carmen from this photo," Jazzman said.

"You don't say." Winston extracted the group photo and held it in his palm. "Any chance we could talk to her?"

"She's only a finger's touch away, my friend." With those words, Jazzman turned to a panel behind him and pressed a red button.

A minute later, a gentle knock at the door sounded. When the nurse entered the room, she gasped. "What did you do, Mr. Jones? I hope you didn't strain yourself."

Jazzman turned to Winston and whispered, "I can't get Madge to use my nickname for the life of me."

The nurse's beady eyes looked at Winston with suspicion. "And who might you be?"

"Don't worry." Jazzman touched Madge's shoulder. "This is a friend of mine, Winston Wong."

Winston extended his hand to Madge, and she shook it with a gentle grip. Everything seemed soft about her, besides those eyes. Her body showed a happy pudginess that traveled from her face down to her feet.

"Jazzman," Winston said, but stopped as Madge's lips quivered at him in irritation. "Mr. Jones, I mean, mentioned that you recognized someone from his old home, Sweet Breeze. Can you point her out in this photo?"

Madge swiveled a round fingertip at Carmen. "This woman. I'm sure of it. Along with her grandmother. Carmen and Eve."

"How did you know them?"

"They came by to check out this home a few months ago. Carmen said she wanted a place downtown. Her grandmother had previously lived nearby and was already comfortable with the area."

"That must have been right before Carmen selected Sweet Breeze for Eve," Jazzman said. "She was a pretty recent resident compared to the rest of us."

"How did she act at Gentle Pastures?" Winston asked Madge. "Anything strange you noticed about her?"

"Carmen seemed skittish. She kept asking about our management and how long we've been in business for." Madge pulled herself to a more upright posture. "We have decades of experience."

"What made her decide against Green Pastures?"

"I'm not sure. Our staff is excellent, and we're well-established in the community."

It sounded like Carmen had investigated the homes before she had committed to Sweet Breeze. Perhaps she had really been looking for one that had an old man tied down to no family, one who wouldn't be readily missed, and Green Pastures didn't offer that opportunity.

Winston fingered the photo of Carmen in the group shot. "Can I take this photo, Jazzman?"

"Be my guest, but take good care of it."

CHAPTER 41

WINSTON GOT INTO his car, stuck his hand in the glove compartment, and fiddled with the contents inside. He pulled out a San Jose map and drew a circle with a five-mile radius extending beyond Green Pastures. He traveled across every main and side street in the area, locating a total of nine senior homes. After checking out each one, Winston confirmed that the striking duo of Eve and Carmen, dowdy grandma and dazzling granddaughter, had made their rounds to four of the sites. The home Winston saved for last ended up being Kristy's current employer, Life Circles.

He saw Kristy as he entered her work place. "What are you doing here?" she asked. She touched the side of his cheek, and he wanted to rest in the comfort of the touch, but he willed himself to move her hand away. "Unfortunately, I'm here on business. It looks like Carmen was checking all the homes within a certain radius before she settled Eve at Sweet Breeze. Could you find out if she visited here as well?"

Kristy pulled out a heavy three-ring binder from a shelf. "No, there's no Eve on the assisted living side." She ran through the pages, licking her finger before flipping each one. He kept watching the flick of her tongue, like a charmed snake, before he realized she'd stopped turning the sheets.

"Did you find something?" he asked.

"There's an Eve Murray who previously lived on the independent side."

"You mean in one of those gleaming townhouse castles?"

"Yes...but the form says she lived at Life Circles only three months before deciding to move in with her granddaughter, Carmen."

"The first names are the same. I'll check it out. Even if it's only a coincidence, at least, I'll get to work side by side with you."

"Tough luck, buddy. I've got to make some rounds. I'll hand you over to Carol on the independent side. She's the activities director over there. I'm sure she'll tell you about Eve Murray in a flash."

Kristy walked him over to another coworker's office. He got to hold her hand for two minutes straight before being passed off. Carol, the activities director, towered over him. She was at least six foot two and her body seemed all lean muscle. "How can I help you, Winston?"

"Have you seen a woman like this at Life Circles?" He pulled out the photo he took from Jazzman's room.

"Of course, I have. That's our very own Eve Murray—right here." She smashed her thumb down on Eve Solstice's printed image. She then pointed to Carmen. "And that's her granddaughter. She visited the home quite often."

"Can you tell me more about Eve Murray?"

"Eve? I remember she was quite the avid baker. Whenever she came to a social event, Eve always brought a treat to share."

"How was she so independent? Didn't she have issues with dementia?"

"I'm not sure. The woman was very quiet, and her granddaughter always hovered over her," Carol said. "I remember that the two of them participated regularly in our book club. We gathered every month with a core of four people, including myself. We had a lively discussion of *White Oleander* right before Eve left. If you want, you can read about it in Julie's minutes."

"Who's Julie?"

"Our book club secretary. She jots down the minutes for the meeting and types them up later. We give them to prospective members to see if they want to join."

"I'd love to take a look at them."

Carol slid out a bulging file folder, extracted a paper and handed it to him. Its flowing, feminine script read:

"Book Club Discussion, *White Oleander*. Attendees: Carol, Eve, Carmen (Eve's granddaughter), Yolanda, and Julie (me).

1. Passed out blueberry scones (another Eve treat) to the group. Delicious with the Earl Grey tea (thank you, Julie).

2. Yolanda started the discussion talking about the Santa Anas. Only two of us have experienced those strong, warm winds.

3. Julie talked about the unfortunate way Ingrid treated Astrid in the book. Murmurs of agreement all around, all of us having been mothers.

4. Yolanda thought that white oleander seemed such a pretty name for a dangerous flower.

5. Carmen wondered how Ingrid thought she could have gotten away with Barry's murder.

6. Carol informed us that there's a plant related to the white oleander called the suicide tree. People use it in India for suicides.

7. Julie asked not to discuss the creepy topic.

8. Yolanda moved on to discuss the foster care system. Lots of headshaking and sighs from everyone.

9. Carol decided to bring up happier subjects and talked about poetry and art, mentioning some mother-daughter creative duos."

So it seemed like Carmen Solstice had learned about poison from her grandmother's book club and the unwitting activities director. How had she moved from head knowledge to physical possession? And how did that all tie back to Rob? Winston needed to go back to the jail again.

CHAPTER 42

BEFORE WINSTON PICKED up the phone, he saw Rob pressing his face up against the glass, like a puppy waiting for its master.

"Got any good news?" Rob fiddled with the collar of his jail uniform. "My trial's only two days away."

"I've got some leads to Carmen, but I'm stuck at a dead end. Maybe you can help me. I need a solid link to tie her to the poison." How had she gotten her hands on the chemical? All the way from India?

Winston recalled Rob's package. "What about that parcel you got from India? Suicide tree grows in abundance there."

Rob shook his head. "All I ordered was a knock-off DS and some bootlegged games." Interesting. Pete *had* mentioned seeing Rob carry around a portable game device with foreign writing on it.

"Nothing else?"

"That and the stupid bracelet I gave to Anastasia. They shipped it to me by mistake."

"There must've been suicide tree in that India shipment somehow. Tell me how you got the knock-off DS."

Rob rubbed his face with his hand. Winston saw dirt clinging to his long half-moon fingernails. "I got the package through Zuras. He knew someone from India and ordered it for me."

"How did Zuras know what to get you?"

"I looked at the goods online."

"Do you remember the URL?"

"Sure, it's www.uniqueindiangoods.com."

Winston scratched at an itch on his neck. It was uncomfortable looking at Rob's probably lice-infested jail shirt.

"Does that help you?" Rob asked. "Can you get me out of here now?"

"I'm not sure about that, but I'm working on it."

Winston left the jail, going east on Hedding and south on Fourth. Seven minutes took him straight to the public library. The King branch of the San Jose library system offered an angular modern exterior with fancy hotel lobby floors and smooth pillars inside. He slid into the seat at an empty computer and typed in his library ID number and password. He accessed the website Rob had told him about and found the ripped-off games and device. Anastasia's bangle was listed on page three of the jewelry listings. When he clicked on the image, he saw other suggested merchandise.

He blinked twice at a familiar image. Flicker. It was like those glitches in the video games, making certain objects transparent and therefore hard to see. He'd missed the significance of the bracelet all along.

That was Carmen's bracelet in the photo; he remembered its distinctive greenish-blue color during the fashion show. The bangle meant that she knew about the Indian website somehow. Maybe she'd seduced the company owner into getting a certain toxin for her. Everything in his investigation linked back to her. He was sure the bracelet held more significance and decided to see Anastasia again.

CHAPTER 43

WINSTON COULDN'T FIND Anastasia in Room 101. Instead, he wandered around peeking through the open doors at Silicon Valley Skilled Nursing Facility for a sight of her fashion-shrouded figure. He found her in a large room, which reminded him of his old elementary school's cafeteria, down to its slippery floors and musty odor. Anastasia sat on a neon green plastic chair, squinting at a bingo card in her hand. Ten other residents lolled around, half of them staring at their numbers and the other half fixated on the man on stage. The slick-haired gentleman rotated a bronze metal cage and pulled out the numbered balls with glacial movements.

"Can I join you, Anastasia?" Winston asked.

"Sure." She breathed out a sigh of relief and handed him the card. "I can't see without my reading glasses, and I'm not letting any of these handsome men look at me in those clunkers."

Winston glanced around. Only two older men sat nearby, one drooling and the other hacking into a stained handkerchief. Not the best of prospects, but beggars couldn't be choosers.

"What did you want?" Anastasia asked.

"I need to update you on the case." Winston caught her up to speed, including Carmen's mysterious link to the Indian-style bracelet.

"Well, I never!" She pulled forth her own bangle and tossed it over to Winston. He caught it but had to juggle the chips on the card to balance it all.

Winston decided to set down the board on Anastasia's lap before he pored over the bracelet. "What's that marking?"

"I never noticed anything before." Anastasia looked around the room with a quick and shrewd glance. Then she pulled out an extremely thick pair of rhinestone-rimmed glasses and put them on. "You're right. There's a line here." She pointed to a crease on it, almost camouflaged by the fancy swirls decorating the piece.

Winston brought the bracelet closer to his face. "It looks like a possible hinge."

"Let me give it a try." Anastasia snatched back her bangle, peering through her lenses and probing for a tiny button. At her furious motions, other people around them stopped playing and started looking their way. Even the announcer glanced over, and a lusty pink colored her wrinkled cheeks. Maybe she wasn't interested in the old geezers, but in the middle-aged *Grease*-wannabe calling out the numbers. Embarrassed, she hid her glasses under the fold of her chiffon dress and passed the bracelet back to Winston.

Winston looked for a tiny knob on the bracelet connected to the hinge, but none appeared, so he banged it against the hard plastic chair. All it evoked was the announcer's gasp of surprise. Beads of sweat rolled down Winston's forehead. *I'll break it if I need to.* He pulled and twisted the thing until it finally made a popping noise. Some contortion of his hand had opened the jewelry. He saw a hollow area inside the bracelet—just big enough for a vial of poison. Winston started whooping.

The announcer stopped his commentating and made his way toward them. "Maybe you can continue this in the hallway. When you're ready to return to the game, Anastasia, please come back alone." He marched them both outside the room, placing a hand on each of their arms.

Anastasia touched the spot on her arm where the man had grabbed her. "He knew my name." She gave a little sigh.

Winston touched her shoulder and held out the bracelet. "This is great, Anastasia."

"Keep it," she said. "For evidence."

"Thanks. I'm that much closer to linking Carmen to the murder."

"Wickedness must pass down through the genes." Anastasia shook her gray head. "Once I saw Eve's tattoo on her leg, I knew about their family's shady past. Maybe it's fortunate that Eve got dementia and blocked out those memories."

"What tattoo are you talking about?"

"Her huge muumuus don't cover her all the time," Anastasia said. "Eve still needed to take the mandatory summer water exercise class at the indoor gym. Nobody else would have noticed the tiny symbol of Prosperity House on her lower right ankle except for someone from the poor side, like me." Anastasia cleared her throat. "But we were all supposed to be from rich backgrounds at Sweet Breeze."

"What's Prosperity House?"

"It's the whorehouse near the projects where I grew up."

Winston couldn't picture bland Eve Solstice as a prostitute.

"Anyone who spent any time in Prosperity House knew trouble with a capital T." Anastasia scribbled down an address for Winston. "Go and check it out, and you'll see what I mean."

CHAPTER 44

PROSPERITY HOUSE, FROM the outside, looked like a run-down shack. Its walls were covered with soot and the wood splintered away from its face. A cloudy window stood half-open, with a crooked sign advertising, "50 cent coffee" in black Mr. Sketch Marker; he could even smell the nasty licorice scent wafting off the ink. Winston called through the half-open sill, and a stooped wizened man ambled over.

"What can I do for you?" The man's features drooped over his body, like a human version of those tripped-out Dali paintings.

"I heard you offer more than coffee here. Is that right?" Winston plunked down a crisp ten-dollar bill.

The old man's eyes seemed to focus on Winston's bare left ring finger. "Looking to warm your bed tonight?"

"No, I just need some information on an old occupant. A private investigation." Winston fished out his business card from his wallet for the old man to inspect.

"Lots of people pass through these doors. What'd she look like?"

Winston whipped out the group photo from Sweet Breeze. He hoped some sort of semblance could be seen even after all her years away from this dump. He handed it over.

The old man pointed straight at Carmen. "It's Doris Winter! Wait, can't be. Doris has been gone for years. And these girl's eyes are brilliant blue." He shook his head a few times. "Shame what happened to her."

"To Doris?"

"Yeah. The Chinese customer—Dragon was his name— knocked her up and ran off. Heard he recently married some rich widow and owns some fancy senior care place now. Broke Doris's heart." The old man ran a shriveled finger down his arm, as though tracing an invisible line. "She OD'd a week after she gave birth."

"What happened to the child?"

He pulled at his white chin stubble, remembering. "Doris had a mother. Retired before my time here. Heard she was as comely as a dishrag. Hardy, though, and that's worth a lot in this line of work. She ran off with the baby after Doris died."

"Did you track her down?"

"Nah. Good riddance. Took care of the problem when it was too late to ask Dr. Wells for help."

"Who's Dr. Wells?"

"Our fine local physician. Walk two blocks that way, and you'll find him." The old man pointed over Winston's left shoulder. "Mobile van with the name of David Wells on it."

"I'm confused. You said he could've helped with the baby. Is he a pediatrician?"

The old man shook his mangy head. "He could've taken care of Doris' situation early on, but her temper used to flare up like those flaming red hairs on her head. She was our star girl, and I couldn't talk her out of giving birth."

"Dr. Wells would've aborted the baby?"

"Sure, he could have. He does everything. He'll suck little bitty babies out, fake diagnoses to get prescription drugs, that sort of thing. If you have the cash."

The doctor seemed a good lead for Winston to follow. The default physician in these parts would have a lot of info. Besides, hadn't Kristy mentioned that Eve's doctor's name started with the letter "D"? Maybe Carmen had turned to David Wells to get the DM-160. If Winston could get the physician's permission, he could link Carmen to the medication and the telltale mark on Joe's body.

Winston shook the old man's hand. "Thanks for talking with me."

"You can thank Mr. Hamilton." The old man folded the greenback and put it away inside a ratty wallet. "He and his presidential buddies can get you anything you want around here."

CHAPTER 45

THE MOBILE VAN was painted an off-red tinge, the better to match the rust stains all around its undercarriage. The lettering, although dry, still seemed to drip because of the painter's sloppy job. The sign read, "Dr. David Wells, Call 1-800-NEED-MED." The windows were painted a dark black all around. Although Winston peered in, he couldn't spy any moving shadows coming from the interior. He knocked on the car doors, and some paint flaked onto his knuckles. He went around back and tried the handles there. A scuffling noise ensued from inside, and the rear doors flung open.

"Hey! What do you think you're doin'?" The man addressing him loomed large, more of a bear than a man. He had curly red hair that sprouted out of every available skin pore. His breath reeked of two days' worth of raw onions.

Winston pointed to the sign on the vehicle's side. "I'm looking for Dr. David Wells."

The man puffed his chest out, looking even more gigantic with the gesture. "That's me."

"You're the doctor?"

"Yeah." David pulled out a cigar from his tan corduroy shirt pocket and lit it. "You got a problem with that?"

"No. I have some questions to ask you." Winston handed over his business card.

"Have a seat." David moved aside a pile of bandages and blood pressure cuffs to reveal a crinkled box labeled, "Syringes with Needles." He motioned for Winston to sit down.

Winston hesitated and then perched on the extreme edge of the cardboard. "Do you remember the name Eve Solstice?"

"I keep track of all my patients in this handy book." David held up a dog-eared journal, one of those blue books used for college exams. At the sight of it, Winston shuddered, remembering how he'd dropped out of community college, much to his parents' shame.

David fiddled with the pages but didn't open up the notebook. In the long pause, Winston sighed and slipped him a twenty. "Now let me see." David flipped the worn pages. "Here's an entry with the name of Solstice. Showed up here several months ago asking for a diagnosis of dementia for her grandmother. Said she couldn't get grandma to leave the house for the diagnosis and asked me to come by, but the wheels on this van are just for show. I got too many regulars to move around for one client, so I took her word for it and gave her an official document."

"Was her name Carmen?"

"Sounds about right. I remember now. She was one hot number." His eyes glazed over, and Winston had to snap his fingers to get David's attention.

"I even told her about a new medication for her grandmother. Me and the pharma rep work real close together." Didn't reps get paid based on sales numbers? Winston could imagine the lucrative deals that were handled in the shady back of this van.

"Was it called DM-160?" Winston asked.

David shrugged. "They're all a bunch of letters and numbers cobbled together. I prescribed it for her, though."

"You have the documentation for that?"

David leaned back on his own box, a shipment of surgical gloves. He kicked his leg against it, denting the flimsy cardboard. "I don't know. That's patient confidentiality rules you're asking me to violate."

Winston gave up another Jackson to feed David's greed.

"I can make you a copy... Here you go, sir. Pleasure doing business with you." Of course, David seemed pleased. Where else could you get a job that paid forty dollars for ten minutes of your time?

Winston looked once into his lonesome wallet where no more bills greeted him. He peered at the paperwork that David had given him—included was the name of a local pharmacy. When he arrived at the large, impersonal drugstore, he pretended to be picking up a prescription for Eve Solstice.

"Date of birth, please," the bored man behind the counter said.

Winston read it off David's notes.

"Still at 217 Laurel Street, Apartment 2A?"

"That's right," Winston said. He jotted down the address.

"Which medication?"

"The DM-160."

The man looked at the computer screen and yawned. "That's out of refills. She picked up the full supply already."

Winston thanked the man and left. He was on the right track, having verified that the DM-160 did get into Carmen's hands. As he was driving away, he decided to take a look at the address he'd been given from the pharmacy. The place was nearby, off of McKee Road.

The brown building faced the roaring main road, the asphalt out front lined with broken glass and cigarette butts. The paint on the walls peeled and curled in on itself, and bars blocked every window in sight. He reached apartment 2A and saw the bright eviction notice taped to the door. The trigger for Carmen's devious plan.

What he didn't know was how to prove that she had given the DM-160 mixed with poison to kill off poor Joe. For that he needed definitive evidence. He had to get into the Solstice household without detection, ideally while Eve and Carmen were both gone.

CHAPTER 46

ONE VISIT TO Alex provided the setup needed to distract Carmen. His friend would lure her away from the house on the premise of viewing the result of her voice acting. To Alex's credit, he did get Carmen a pretty prime spot in *Women Warriors*. Her sultry voice lent sex appeal to a fiery redhead named Sasha. Decked in leather, the avatar looked like Red Sonja from *Conan the Barbarian*.

Winston listened in as Alex called Carmen and invited her over for the next day. Alex insisted that Carmen bring her grandmother to the mini fête, so she could see Carmen's success first-hand. Winston could picture the party already. The food would consist of buffalo wings and pizza. The company: game developers, salivating at the chance to meet the screen babe they'd created, in real life.

* * *

The event was scheduled for 1:00 p.m., so Winston pulled up to the new Solstice residence at twenty past the appointed hour. He figured it was enough time to compensate for typical "fashionably late" diva tardiness. He slipped into the front door with the key he'd made during the recording session.

In the living room, he examined the flat screen TV closer. Instead of an American brand, he saw Hindi writing on it. At least, he knew how the Solstices could afford new technology on their budget—from their Indian contact.

A pale glow illuminated the space, and he could see an Apple laptop resting on the piano lid. The screensaver played glamour shots of Carmen, ranging from moderately unclothed to almost nude. Winston pressed down on the keypad, and the computer resumed. The screen was logged into *Space Domination*—with the user name of Zuras. Carmen's comment to Alex about being an avid gamer flashed in Winston's head. It all clicked together like a key in a lock. Carmen had used the Zuras handle to goad Rob into finishing off Joe.

She had hoped to find a pliant puppet in Rob. Maybe she had wanted him to complete the task himself to keep her hands clean, but when he balked, she decided to step in.

Winston still needed concrete evidence not theories, though. He knew where to start and walked toward Joe's old room once more. He pulled the handle and opened the door into a slew of mess. Chest drawers hung open, tidy linens transformed into quilt heaps, and crumpled papers littered the floor. Somebody had trashed the place.

Winston started looking in all the crevices and under the bed. All he got in return was a string of sneezes. As his last "ah-choo" subsided, he heard a loud click from the front of the house. Arguing voices could be heard through Joe's open bedroom door.

"Oh come on, Nana. It's not every day that I get to be part of a video game. Why did you make me turn the car around?" He heard the pout in Carmen's voice even from this distance.

"You didn't tell me this new project of yours came from a favor from Winston Wong until we got through the door."

"Whatever. The man's harmless. He never figured out that I was cheating the system."

"I don't want you indebted to him, Carmen. Now help me find that DM-160 tube."

"It's gotta be here somewhere, Nana. I looked for it plenty the day you lost it."

"I just don't like my things missing."

"You and your order. It's not like you need to use the medicine anyway."

"Wait a minute, the computer still has *Space Domination* running. Why isn't the screen saver on? We've been gone long enough. It should have kicked in automatically."

"I don't know, and I don't care, Nana. I'm not letting you ruin a celebration party for me. I'll go by myself." He could hear Carmen storm out of the house.

Winston looked at the open door to Joe's old room. If Eve walked a little farther on in the house, she'd spot it right away, and he didn't think he could close it without attracting her attention. He couldn't walk back out the way he'd entered either.

He scrambled to the patio door and yanked it open. The hinges squealed like a pig on steroids. He made it through but heard the sound of footsteps coming closer.

He ran even faster and squished himself into the bush that blocked the way to the back garden. He got caught in its numerous branches, though, and felt an iron hand grip his foot. "Stop right there, Winston," Eve said.

CHAPTER 47

WINSTON TRIED TO yank his foot away from Eve's grasp. He flailed at her, feeling as useless as when he button-mashed an old arcade game. Eve's fingers loosened a tad but found some traction on his flip-flops and his knobby toes. He decided to distract her by engaging in conversation. At least, that tactic worked in the movies. "I know you're cheating the system, Miss-Fake-Dementia."

She chuckled. "You still don't understand, do you?"

"I know that Rob didn't kill Joe, and I intend to prove his innocence."

"Rob was a great scapegoat. I liked chatting with him through *Space Domination*."

"Wait, you're Zuras?"

"Now you're getting it."

"How did you have access to the game at Sweet Breeze?"

"My trusty tablet. You saw Carmen borrowing it that day on the back patio. Didn't you see my logo on it?" The woman with the serpent around the Apple symbol: Eve.

"Where did you keep that hidden?"

"Used my typical attire." She patted her giant heart-covered muumuu. "I keep all my important stuff near me." She flashed it open, and he saw the hidden inner pocket—with a pair of rainbow fuzzy socks nestled inside.

He needed to continue talking and keep her occupied. "I saw the figure-eight mark on Joe's body. Why use the DM-160 at all?" Winston snapped a branch off the bush for a weapon, but the soft bark curled up in his hand.

"That happened when Plan A failed. I had already put the poison in the dialysis bags in the cabinet while people were distracted during Anastasia's birthday party. Easy to do since I'm always 'wandering.' But then Rob had to be a hero and cut the bags.

"I knew the poison would drain out before Joe was affected, so I went to Joe's room to finish the job. The extra boost from the DM-160 would make the poison stronger. I needed it to act fast, so I could grab his lucky socks."

"He saw you," Winston said. "Anastasia heard him talking to somebody."

"He managed only a few words before I mixed the primer with the remaining toxin and injected him with it."

Winston eyed the bush near him. He pulled the leaves back, increasing their tension, hoping for the plant to spring into Eve's face. Instead, it struck him on his left cheek, and he winced. "But Joe was a friend of yours. A fellow resident."

Eve's eagle talons seemed to slice into his big toe as she spoke. "They're all pawns to me: Rob, Joe."

"Tell me something. How do you even get a batch of suicide tree?"

"Connections from past customers."

"That reminds me. Tell me about your daughter, Doris." Eve's hand slipped then, and Winston tried to pull away, but she held onto the teeniest fraction of his heel. "You let her grow up in a whorehouse, use drugs, even OD."

"No, not true. Dragon drove her to her death."

"But Doris was the one using drugs."

"It's a rough life," Eve said with a sigh. "You never grew up in the projects. It's so hard to get out of there."

"But didn't you marry Teddy and leave?"

Eve spat at him and missed his face by a few inches to the left. "That was all a ruse."

"How did you have a daughter then?"

"The same way Doris did. Who do you think would ever marry a whore?"

"But the photo at Joe's funeral?"

"The sample picture that comes with the frame." Anastasia had been right about that. "No husbands for us. Although we didn't have anybody but ourselves to rely on, Doris still insisted on having the baby. Stubborn girl." She said the words without malice, and a tiny smile even appeared on her face.

"So then you raised Doris's daughter, Carmen. Like grandmother, like granddaughter, huh? You and Carmen did Joe in together."

Eve snarled at him then. "My granddaughter's innocent of murder. I told you before. Family is everything to me."

"Carmen's the only family you have. Do you mean you killed Joe for her?"

"In a way. I knew Dragon owned some sort of residential care facility near downtown—somebody Facebooked about it—but couldn't figure out the exact name. He doesn't deserve to be a successful businessman, rich only by ditching my daughter and marrying up.

"It was a two-for-one deal. With a murder on his hands, his reputation would falter. And my granddaughter's always wanted a grand home like this." Winston thought back to the day on the back patio when he discussed Carmen's modeling career and what she wanted to buy with the money. "I managed to get her the exact one she wanted. With his Chinese superstitions, I realized he'd sell a house where there had been a murder."

"Carmen must have known something."

"Winston, my granddaughter may be well-endowed, but it's not in the brains department. All she did was follow my suggestion of getting a fake dementia diagnosis. That was so she could get the grant money."

"She was scouting out old people's homes with you, though, looking for a victim."

"No, I couldn't afford Life Circles much longer. My savings was going away, and I knew Carmen couldn't support me. Besides, a senior home would make my dementia story even more believable."

"You two came together to see me at my office, so that I could eventually frame Rob."

"Right. I wanted to create a huge scandal. But keep Carmen out of this. I told her that I suspected some foul play. She knew nothing about how it actually happened. All she did was find your sorry name in the *Pennysaver*."

Eve dropped her grip on his foot then and lunged at his throat. He contorted his body in a twist and kicked out. Startled by the movement, she fell backwards. Meanwhile, Winston landed facedown and army-crawled through the hedge. He made it to the back patio and clambered over a side gate.

Winston puffed his way to his car and sped off to Life Circles. There, Kristy stared in surprise at his crazy state. While she bound his big toe, bleeding from a deep gash, he relayed his exploits at the Solstice home.

After he finished talking, Kristy said, "I keep thinking about that wrecked room."

"Pete did mention that he saw Carmen scrutinizing the floor the day of Joe's death. Probably looking for that missing DM-160 tube."

"If Eve hasn't found it yet, there might be someone else who spotted it first." She tapped against the box of bandages, forgotten in her hand. "Let me take some time off and join you on a little trip."

CHAPTER 48

HAROLD MEEKINGS LAY motionless on his hospital bed in the crowded living room. Bookshelves towered above him, filled with a wide array of books, from beach reads to yawn-inducing tomes. A curio display holding exquisite chinaware stood to one side. A bubbling fish tank in another corner covered the strain of his labored breathing.

Tubes seemed to run at all angles around Harold, entombing him in curlicues of plastic. His eyes were closed, his cheeks sunken, and his lips parched. Winston saw that his skin had turned an odd yellowish tinge. Harold's relatives stood on the periphery of the room or peered from the kitchen through the cut-out archway. A hospice nurse flitted in and out of the scene.

Winston edged closer to the bed. "Hello, Mr. Meekings. It's Winston from Sweet Breeze. Do you remember me?" The faintest rise of Harold's chest answered Winston. "I'm still working on that case that Kristy told you about. Did you find anything odd in the room where you stayed?"

No emotion crossed Harold's face. Winston tried several times, and even touched the man, but shrank back as his hand brushed against the coldness of Harold's fingertips.

Winston felt a touch on his shoulder from Kristy. He moved back to let her try.

"Harold? It's me, Kristy. I'm glad that you're able to be with your family now, and I know that the nurses from Serenity Hospice are all very sweet and professional." Winston saw Kristy hold Harold's hand without a shiver at its iciness. "It would really help us if you could give us any information. Remember, I told you about poor Joe who used to be in the same room as you?" Harold's eyes blinked, and his mouth seemed to move a tiny fraction. Kristy leaned closer, her ear brushing against his dry mouth. She looked back at Winston with a frown. He knew she hadn't been able to decipher any words.

"How about this, Harold? If you want to say, 'yes,' you can blink. Otherwise, remain still. Did you find anything in Joe's room?"

A quiver of the lids.

"Is it still at Sweet Breeze?" Nothing.

"Is the item here?" A tremble of an eyelash.

"Where is it?" No movement from the eyes, but then a gnarled finger rose, slowly, to point in the direction of the bookcase.

Harold seemed spent from that small physical exertion. "It's in a book?" Kristy moved toward the open shelves. Winston joined her and saw her run a finger across the titles, inviting a trail of dust to cover her hand. "He loved mysteries, especially by Agatha Christie. I think *And Then There Were None* was his favorite." She picked up the tome and flipped through it. Nothing fell from the pages. Kristy rapped on the spine and tried to peek underneath the covers, but even from his angle, Winston could see that the book was solid. A grim line surfaced on Kristy's face. "I thought we were onto something."

Winston felt frustrated that he'd wasted his time. He looked at the rows of books and wanted to knock over the whole tower.

Something caught his eye during his mental rampage. A glint of silver. He reached into the hollow behind where the book had rested and seized upon an object in its shadows. A tube, labeled DM-160 with the name "Eve Solstice" printed in bold black letters. He tilted it from side to side and could hear the slosh of a few precious liquid drops inside.

* * *

Kristy contacted Officer Gaffey, and they met at The Jukebox Café. Three orders of coffee, but only the cop asked for the meatloaf special. Winston couldn't find the stomach to eat, excitement for once overtaking his need for food. Kristy, he could see, kept spinning her cup around, a sign of her nervousness.

Officer Gaffey spooned a forkful of moist meat into his mouth. "So what are we here for?"

Winston and Kristy started talking over one another, but Officer Gaffey interrupted them. "The same case? You two work on this as a team?"

Kristy looked at Winston and gave him a little smile. She placed her hand on top of his on the sticky dining table. "Yes, we did it *together*."

Winston watched Officer Gaffey's lips quiver before he cleared his throat. Winston: 1, Officer Gaffey: 0. "Okay, then. Tell me what you found out."

They led him along the investigative trail. They talked about Eve faking her dementia diagnosis, hunting for elderly housing, using Rob as a scapegoat, and injecting a combo dosage of DM-160 and suicide tree into Joe's body, all to exact revenge on her daughter's old lover.

Officer Gaffey dropped his jaw and pushed his nearly full plate of food away. "Are you serious?"

Winston pulled out the customized DM-160 container and handed it over. "Have the fancy police lab run some tests."

Gaffey touched the tube with an outstretched finger and shook his head. "That poor Joe Sawyer."

"What do you think will happen at the trial?" Winston asked.

"Hopefully, justice will be served."

CHAPTER 49

One week later...

WINSTON LOOKED AT the front page article. "Grandmother Charged with Murder," the headline read. The poison found in the DM-160 tube and Eve's subsequent confession had given the jury no doubt about her involvement. He heard from Kristy that Harold had passed shortly after providing the crucial evidence. Harold's family said that he'd died with a broad smile across his face.

Winston studied the photo attached to the newsprint. Eve, even through the camera lens, seemed to emit ice through her eyes. He shivered and put the newspaper away.

After Eve's arrest, Rob had been released from jail. The last he'd heard, Rob was the spokesperson for *Space Domination*, his famous face gathering even more players to the massive online game. He was well on his way to breaking into the industry for sure.

Carmen started going steady with his friend Alex and had moved into his apartment. Alex told Winston that he was inundated with calls for her voice acting. She'd even been offered a role in the latest eroge. This new income would help her pay off the large fine she'd gotten from the local nonprofit for taking their dementia grant under false pretenses. Alex also informed Winston that she had started on a memoir entitled, *My Nana the Murderer.*

A stack of phone messages lay in Winston's "To Do" tray. Gossip of his brilliant sleuthing had already made the rounds in the various senior centers the Sweet Breeze residents had eloped to. He thought about his Sweet Breeze friends:

Anastasia liked her time at Silicon Valley Skilled Nursing. All the other residents treated her with respect, and she even shed some of her gauzy princess wrappings to move around with greater ease.

Jazzman found a surprise waiting for him after Eve's arrest— an upright piano delivered to Gentle Pastures. He kept his fellow residents happy with jazzy tunes. Sometimes he'd get a faraway look, though, and play a classical piece.

Pete joined a support group at the veterans' hospital. He befriended some folks there, dropped solitaire, and organized enormous card-playing events.

Winston flipped through the notes from the potential clients in the tray but chose to let them sit there. The cases would have to wait. He whipped out his pocket comb and straightened his remaining hair strands. He patted his belly and sighed. His sister Marcy had teased him again during their recent videoconferencing session, the first in a series of planned monthly virtual meetings.

He blamed his enduring pooch on Kristy and their eating out together. Today he would take his girlfriend out for real this time, sans any casework, to a local barbecue place. It boasted peanut shells on the floor and an oven the size of a truck to smoke their famous ribs.

Before he left the office, Winston snatched one of his new business cards from his faux gold holder to show Kristy. The order had arrived yesterday. The crisp cardboard pieces with an emblem of a magnifying glass read, "Winston Wong, Seniors' Sleuth."

ACKNOWLEDGEMENTS

First off, to you readers: A very big 7h4nk y0u! If you enjoyed this book, please leave a kind review.

Warmest wishes to San Jose natives and residents who let me stage a murder in their city and rearrange their streets.

Also, my gratitude goes out to a superb editor, Alicia Street, for attention to major and minor details. I am extremely indebted to the lovely writers who supported me through their blurbs: Sarah M. Chen, Gay Degani, Hannah Dennison, Naomi Hirahara, and Lois Lavrisa. (A very special thanks goes out to Hannah who first took me under her professorial wing.)

Thank you to first readers, Ekta Nair and Christine Su. A hearty round of applause for my SB Writers' Group. I also want to give a shout-out to the members of Team Jen: Carol Early Cooney, Rosa Fontana, Monica Frazier, Enna Lee-McNeil, Jane Ann McLachlan, Emma Mejia, Joy Weese Moll, Janice Sheridan, and Julia Tomiak.

And, of course, to my fantastic husband, Steve, who not only gave me technical advice, but also read through multiple drafts of this novel: I <3 you.

Made in the USA
San Bernardino, CA
29 February 2020